JUST BEYOND
THOSE HILLS

Also by Alan Hilfiker

POETRY
Sources Of The Morning
Finding Other Countries
Searching For Azaleas

STORY POEMS
Memorial Day

SHORT STORIES
Journeys Off The Road

CHILDREN'S STORIES
Once Upon A Times

FICTION
Bareback On A Unicorn

JUST BEYOND THOSE HILLS

Alan Hilfiker

Elmcroft Publications

The content associated with this book is the sole work and responsibility of the author. Gatekeeper Press had no involvement in the generation of this content.

Just Beyond Those Hills

Published by Gatekeeper Press
7853 Gunn Hwy., Suite 209
Tampa, FL 33626
www.GatekeeperPress.com

Copyright © 2024 by Alan Hilfiker

All rights reserved. Neither this book, nor any parts within it may be sold or reproduced in any form or by any electronic or mechanical means, including information storage and retrieval systems, without permission in writing from the author. The only exception is by a reviewer, who may quote short excerpts in a review.

The cover design and editorial work for this book are entirely the products of the author. Gatekeeper Press did not participate in and is not responsible for any aspect of these elements.

Library of Congress Control Number: 2024939403

ISBN (paperback): 9781662952081

DEDICATION

To Elizabeth "Libby" Horn
1937 – 2023

ACKNOWLEDGEMENTS

I wish to thank the following individuals for helping me with respect to these stories and story poems.

My daughter, Marjorie Markart, for her guidance and editorial assistance.

Amy Fox Dangler, for her patience, skill, and cheerful endurance preparing so many drafts and revisions.

And especially, Elizabeth A. Horn, ("Libby") for her inspiration, edits, and factual references for *My Uncle Sal.*

TABLE OF CONTENTS

PART ONE: SHORT STORIES ... 1

    FROM THE DIARY OF GUENTHER HOETTL ... 2

    THE BIRDFEEDER ... 7

    THE SLAVER'S SON-IN-LAW ... 14

    THE ASSASSIN ... 19

    MY UNCLE SAL ... 76

    THE RUSSIAN DESERTER ... 99

    THE CONFESSION OF OBERLEUTNANT HELMUT PRAHL ... 127

    TWO SETS OF HANDS ... 135

PART TWO: STORY-POEMS ... 137

    RAIN ... 138

    GRACIE ... 148

    BLACK ... 163

    BUTTERFLIES ... 170

PART ONE:
SHORT STORIES

FROM THE DIARY OF GUENTHER HOETTL

October 5, 1943
Dubno, Ukraine

At about 15:45 hours, I drove my truck to the site. It was near two great mounds of earth dug up as an anti-tank ditch. Now the ditch served another purpose.

My truck was crammed full. Mostly, the cargo was Jews, but there were some Bolsheviks mixed in. There were men, women, and children of all ages.

The Ukrainian militia herded them off my truck. Most got off and did what they were told. But some of them resisted. Those, the Ukrainians struck with rifle butts. Others were kicked and punched. One Jew was whipped by Franz until his shirt was ripped to shreds and his back was raw. Outside the truck, the Jew dropped to the ground and cowered there and wouldn't move. Then Franz whipped him some more. He still didn't cooperate. So Franz shot him in the face.

I stood by and watched.

A few seconds later, a young Pole in his teens—Bolshevik and not a Jew—tried to escape. He ran toward the woods. He got within 20 meters of the trees before I shot him. Those were our orders: shoot any who don't cooperate, resist, or try to escape.

I went up to him. To where he was lying. He was still twitching. Probably just nerves. I shot him again just to be sure. In the back of the head. He didn't twitch after that. Then I ordered two Ukrainians to drag him to the ditch and throw him in. I told them to be careful not to let him shield any Jews who might still be alive.

After that, we got the remaining cargo lined up and marched them to the base of the mound. The mound was in front of the ditch. It blocked the view of the ditch. But I think some of the Jews knew what was behind the mound.

We made them undress. Told them to place their clothes in separate piles: outer clothes in one pile, underclothes in another, shoes in still another. There was a heap of shoes. Perhaps 800 to 1,000 pairs. Great piles of clothes and underwear. These might be usable by the folks back home. Clothing and shoes were in short supply for them. Times were tough for our people.

Without screaming or weeping these people undressed, stood around in family groups, kissed each other, said farewells, and waited for a sign from another of our men. Reinhard, I think he was. He stood near the end of the mound. He, too, had a whip. A "cat-o'-nine-tails" I think they call it.

During the 15 minutes I stood there, I heard no complaint or plea for mercy from the Jews. They were passive and didn't resist. Perhaps they were just too weak and starved. Some, perhaps, were relieved that their suffering soon would be over. Those who knew, those who'd lost all hope.

I watched a family of eight people. A man and a woman both about 50. Children about one, eight and ten years old, and two grown-up daughters in their 20s. Also an old woman. Probably one of the grandmothers. She had snow-white hair, and she was holding the one-year-old in her arms, singing to it and tickling it. The child was cooing with delight. The couple was looking on with tears in their eyes. The father was holding the hand of a 10-year-old boy and speaking to him softly. The boy was fighting back tears. The father pointed to the sky and stroked his head. He seemed to explain something to him.

At that moment, the SS-man at the pit shouted something to Reinhard, who counted off about 20 people and instructed them to go behind the earth mound. Among them was the family I just mentioned. I well remember one of the daughters, slim and with black hair, who, as she passed close to me, pointed to herself, and said "23." At the time, I thought perhaps she might have been set aside for the officers.

But someone must have decided she wasn't good enough. On second glance, I could see why. Too thin. Too boney. Perhaps she'd have been selected if she hadn't lost so much weight at the camp.

Then I walked around the mound and saw the huge, common grave. Bodies were lying on top of one another. Like filets of fish in a tin. Like a stack of cord wood. One layer on top of another. Too many layers to count. The pit was quite deep. There was blood running over all of them. Like a sort of gravy.

Some of the people who'd been shot were still moving. Some were lifting their arms and turning their heads. Showing they were still alive. The pit was already two-thirds full. I estimated that it already contained about 1,000 people.

I looked for the man who did the shooting. It was Emil. He sat on the edge of the pit. His feet dangled into it. It was his break. He had a machine gun on his lap and he was reloading it. A cigarette stuck out of his mouth. Smoke coiled upward from the cigarette and made him squint. There was smoke still coming from the muzzle of his machine gun. That smoke also stung his eyes.

The people, completely naked, were ordered to walk down some steps which were cut in the clay wall of the pit. The SS-men directed them down. They were ordered to walk over the people who were lying there and then lie down themselves. Some of the people they walked over were still alive, but most of them were dead. Layers of people as I said. I don't know how many layers.

The new people did as they were told. They lay down on top of the dead and the wounded. Some caressed those who were still alive and spoke to them in a low voice. Then Emil started shooting again.

His break was over.

I looked into the pit and saw that some of the bodies were twitching. Mostly, though, they were lying motionless on top of the bodies which lay below them. Blood was running down their shoulders and necks.

All the time he was shooting, Emil was smoking. The cigarette hung at an angle from his lips. When he finished shooting, he flicked his cigarette into the pit. It sizzled for a moment in the blood of one of the corpses. Then it went out.

I turned and went back to my truck. When I got back to it, Horst's truck had already arrived. The Ukrainians were starting to unload its cargo. Horst was now finished for the day. I still had one more load to get from the camp before it got dark.

The days were getting shorter now.

I knew I had to hurry on account of the darkness."

Note: "Guenther Hoettl", "Franz", "Reinhard", "Emil" and "Horst" are fictional characters who represent members of the Einstat Special Action SS forces, Group Four, of the Nazis, who were stationed in Ukraine in World War II.

Although the names of the characters are fictional, the events described, nevertheless, appallingly, were real. They are set forth in a report of one Hermann Graebe, a German manager and engineer in charge of a branch office of the Josef Jung firm in Zdolbuniv, Ukraine. The text of his report appears in Whitney R. Harris' book about the Nuremberg trials entitled "Tyranny on Trial", Revised Edition, Southern Methodist University Press, 1999 at pp. 357-58. Graebe observed the events on that day, but only as a witness, not as an active participant in this atrocity as I have depicted.

THE BIRDFEEDER

Trudi sat in her wheelchair staring out her window at the Heritage Springs Nursing Home. She was staring at the bird feeder just outside.

It was a brightly colored, cheerful looking bird feeder shaped like a little house with four open sides. It had a brilliant blue floor—the tray for the birdseed—with half-inch high sides to hold the seeds and on which the visiting birds could perch. Four little pillars—spindles, real—one orange, one purple, one green, and one pink—supported a sunny yellow roof. A perky little red chimney topped the ridgeline, and several brightly colored flowers were painted on its slopping sides. It hung from a hook on a long metal rod which squirrels couldn't climb, denying them access to the birdseed they craved.

Altogether, it was quite an attractive little thing, nodding in just the slightest of breezes, and when birds abruptly landed.

All sorts of birds came to the feeder. Cardinals—males, bright red with contrasting black bibs under their beaks—followed by their contrasting drab brown mates. Blue jays: blue and gray and black. Pesky little sparrows and grackles, with their glossy, black, iridescent plumage and sharp black beaks. Mourning doves, much too large for the little house, who, when they landed scattered birdseed onto the ground. Every so often, a brightly colored goldfinch, matching the color of the roof, swooped down to pay a visit.

At first, Trudi tried to name the birds. That worked for a couple of days and then doubts set in, particularly with the sparrows. Several often came together and how, she wondered, could she be sure the birds she'd carefully named the day before—even just minutes before—were the ones that now arrived. So, reluctantly, she gave up trying to name the birds.

Except for one that she couldn't fail to recognize. It was clearly distinct from all the others. A male cardinal, slightly larger than the other males, Trudi thought, and perhaps a dash of red more colorful. He was different from the other cardinals in one other respect as well. In fact, he was different from any other bird Trudi had ever seen before: he only had one leg.

This one she named "Charlie," after her husband who'd been dead for sixteen years. His picture was on her bedside table and the ring he'd slipped upon her finger seventy-eight years ago was still upon her finger. Heaven help the aide who tried to take it off.

She named him "Charlie" for a multitude of reasons: Because Charlie had been her lifelong partner. (They had raised their three kids, Tom, Liz and Mary Beth together.)

And because of their shared struggles. Each had worked two jobs to keep the household solvent. He, his day job on the "A" shift from 8:00 a.m. to 4:00 p.m. at the GM plant, then nights as custodian from 5:30 to 9:30 at Comerica Bank. She, at the high school cafeteria from 10:00 a.m. to 3:00 p.m.; and before and after that, the world's most important job as Charlie called it: being a "mom" and doing all the things a mom must do.

Part One: Short Stories

And because he'd never cheated. He'd always been faithful. This she knew for certain. As certain as she knew the same about herself. And, because she knew that if he ever had strayed, he would have told her. "He would have 'fessed up right afterwards because he couldn't have stood it otherwise," she told her friends with absolute certainty and confidence.

And because of the war. The one thing they never talked about. The Korean war. The Inchon landing. The Chinese horde that cut off Charlie's regiment from the rest of the U.S. troops in the dead of winter. When the temp was thirty-six below. The fact that his regiment had been written off by generals at the Pentagon. Written off, too, by all the newspapers. Even by Huntly-Brinkley and Walter Cronkite. But not by Colonel Wier. Not by Colonel Ben Wier, Charlie's commanding officer. He hadn't given up. He hadn't abandoned hope. He'd resolved that somehow; he'd get his troops out. That he'd will them out. And somehow, he did. Against all odds, somehow, he did. But not without losses. Not without those who had to be carried out—some in body-bags, some severely wounded. Like Charlie. Like Charlie hobbling through the ice and snow on crutches. One legged Charlie. A leg he'd lost to frostbite at thirty-six below.

That's why she named the cardinal "Charlie."

What other name would do?

*

Trudi's room at Heritage Springs was spare and bleak. Depressingly spare and bleak, but it was all she could afford. It was all that Medicaid would pay for after the proceeds from the sale of her double-wide had run out.

The walls of her room were barren, pictureless. Except for one. A cheap print of a winter scene permanently hung on the wall behind her bed. That was it. Nothing else adorned her walls. Photographs and paintings would have to be hung on hooks, and hooks required nails, and nails made holes; and, many times, the residents at Heritage Springs weren't there that long. That would lead to too many holes. So, photos or paintings that residents might want hung on their walls were not allowed.

The only other decorative item was a vase of plastic geraniums on her dresser. Except for a small photograph of Charlie and Trudi, framed, and standing on her little bedside table, that was it.

But Trudi did have her window and the bird feeder. *Thank goodness for my window and the bird feeder,* Trudi often thought.

And then there was the home itself. That, too, was depressing. The sounds outside her door. The moans, the screams, the pleas for help. The TV in a neighbor's room turned up much too loud. Turned up too loud because her neighbor was hard of hearing. Couldn't hear her soaps and the endless bray of game show hosts. But Trudi did. Trudi clearly did. Whether she wanted to or not. And mostly she did not.

There were other sounds too. Also depressing. Sounds of 911 crews wheeling someone in or wheeling someone out. Sounds of wailing ambulances arriving and departing with grim cargo. But the most depressing sounds of all came from across the hall. The screams of

Part One: Short Stories

Mrs. Wilford. "Help! Help! Help!" she'd scream at the slightest inconvenience. The most modest of misfortunes. Like when she dropped a Kleenex, or when she wanted her TV channel changed, or an extra blanket. She never pushed her buzzer. Never turned her hall light on. Instead, she chose to scream. Always it was "Help! Help! Help! Someone, please! Someone help!"

The visuals weren't good either. Especially the line of residents in their wheelchairs outside the dining room at mealtime. They, with their marbled-mucous eyes and gaping mouths queued in the hallway waiting. Waiting for their dinners. Waiting for their ends to come.

*

Today it was raining. It was cold and hardly any birds had come to the feeder. "November," Trudi said out loud to herself, "perhaps, they've all flown south." Nevertheless, Trudi stayed at the window looking out past the bird feeder to the leafless trees and the hedge rimming the property line and obscuring its chain-link fence. The chain-link fence which assured Heritage Springs that none of its residents, who did manage to get out of the building, would stray off the property.

*

Yesterday had been Trudi's birthday. Her 98th. She'd had brief calls from Tom and Liz. Tom's call lasted two minutes—he was on his way to a meeting with his broker. ("I'd like to talk longer, Mom, but I'm running a bit late. I'll call you later," he said. But never did.)

Liz's call was a bit longer. Perhaps five minutes. But hers, too, was cut short. She was grocery shopping and was approaching the checkout line. "Anyway, Mom, have a great day" was how she closed. And her third child, Mary Beth: she never even bothered to call.

Trudi did, however, receive two cards from her family, one from Liz and one from her great granddaughter, Emily, Liz's granddaughter. It was a handmade card probably made at school with crayons on plain white paper. Emily had printed her name in large, awkward, capital letters across the bottom half of the paper. Emily was five and had just started kindergarten. There was also a card from the nursing home staff. It was the same card they'd given her the year before.

*

Trudi shut off her TV. She'd heard enough from CNN's experts about the missing plane and all its Chinese passengers, Malaysian Air Flight 370. All she wanted now was silence. Dinner wouldn't be for an hour yet.

She wheeled herself closer to the window and rested her frail, wrinkled arms on the sill.

It was starting to get dark. The rain had stopped, but Trudi knew it was still quite cold. She'd heard the weather forecast and they advised the temperature might drop into the twenties. "Quite cold," the pert, young meteorologist said. "It might even snow. Perhaps a prewinter dusting. A harbinger of things to come."

Part One: Short Stories

Suddenly there was a flutter of red outside the window. It was Charlie. He flew quite close to the window; and, despite having only one leg, landed deftly on the roof of the bird feeder, his red nearly matching that of the little chimney.

Charlie cocked his head from side to side, then turned toward Trudi's window seeming to look inside, directly at Trudi. Seeming to stare at her as she was staring at him. For several seconds they held each other's gaze. Neither moved nor blinked.

Then Charlie, cocking his head and looking to his left toward the hedge at the property line, took off. He flew in swoops and glided over the lawn, over the hedge, over the fence and was gone.

Gone to the west. Gone toward the setting sun.

Trudi watched him fly away. Watched him fly above the hedge, above the chain-link fence, watched him until he disappeared.

*

"Help! Help! Help! Someone, please help!" Mrs. Wilford screamed from across the hall.

This time she couldn't find her glasses.

They were on the table next to where she was sitting.

"Help! Help! Help!" she screamed again.

This time even louder.

Trudi remained at her window staring out across the lawn, over the hedge and over the chain-link fence.

"Oh, how I wish I could fly away like him," she said.

"Oh, how I wish he'd take me with him."

THE SLAVER'S SON-IN-LAW

Charleston, South Carolina
August 14, 1803

Wife: "You look tired, Milton."

Husband: "I am. I admit it. I am."

Wife: "Why, what happened?"

Husband: "Your father's ship. *The Coursan* . . ."

Wife: "Yes...what about it? Did it founder? Was it lost at sea?"

Husband: "No . . . no . . . nothing like that. It would have been better if it had been lost . . . it had sunk."

Wife: "So it didn't sink? It made it to port safely?"

Husband: "Yes, it arrived safely. But . . ."

Wife: "But what?"

Husband: "It was horrible. Horrible what I saw. The ship had been at sea for 17 days.

There were over 500 captured Africans onboard. Fifty-five had already been thrown overboard.

"The Africans were crowded into three decks below the main deck. Each deck was only 3 feet 3 inches high. They were packed together so tight that the Africans were sitting upright between one another's legs.

Part One: Short Stories

Everyone was completely nude. There was no possibility of their lying down or changing their position at all. Night or day.

"Each one had been branded. Burnt with the red-hot iron on their breast or arm. Many were children, little girls and little boys.

"Light could not reach down into the bowels of the ships. Neither could fresh air. The heat and stench were so great and so offensive it was a miracle that any survived. But some did.

"These people, these human beings, sat in their own vomit, urine and feces, and that of the others crammed in with them as well. If another person sat between your legs, their bowels emptied out on you.

"Many women onboard experienced menstruation.

"Many of the enslaved who were sick or driven mad were simply thrown overboard with chains on them to drag them down. To be sure they'd drown. Others simply jumped. In fact, there was so much human flesh going over the side of those ships that sharks learned to trail them.

"And then for those who survived the journey across the ocean, they were put on the trading block and auctioned off. I mean families were split up. Husbands and wives were sold to different owners. Little children separated from their parents, their mothers.

"Supposing we were on the block instead of them? Supposing we were sold off? Separated from one another? And our kids torn away from us.

"Awful . . . it was awful . . . horrible. You could see the pain on their faces. You could feel their pain, their anguish.

"I don't think I can take it any longer, Martha. It's not right. It's not right what your father's doing. In fact, it's immoral . . . the teachings of Christ!"

Wife: "But it's his business. It's the family's business. My Grandfather Bertram started it. Before the Revolution. And it's been very profitable. It's enabled us to live in this house. This mansion. And we treat our slaves well. Feed them. Give them good quarters compared to those who go to the plantations."

Husband: "I know. I know, Martha. But the ordeal of the voyages. I just can't abide that anymore. I've got to do something else."

Wife: "What? What are you thinking of?"

Husband: "I don't know exactly. When I was at Cambridge, I knew a chap named Randall Scott. He's in Bedford, Massachusetts. His father owns a whaling fleet. We were pretty close at school. He might persuade his father to take me on. I could be an exporter . . . you know . . . shipments of oil to other parts of the country . . . to England or to France . . . ."

Wife: "But you'd have to live up there."

Husband: "Yes, I know. We'd have to move."

Wife: "I'd never go, Milton. Never . . . ever . . . never ever would I go. I'm not leaving this house. This city. My parents. No. No. Banish the thought. I'm not leaving this life! You'll have to leave without me. Without the children. And I won't hear of it. You'll have to leave on your own if you feel that strongly about it."

Husband: "It's wrong Martha. The cargo your father is importing isn't things. It's people. They're humans like us. Human beings. Families like ours. Husbands. Wives. Mothers. Fathers. Little children. They're like us, Martha."

Wife: "They're not like us. They're different. They're animals that resemble us, but they're more like apes. They're subhuman. Don't say they're like us. Because they're not."

Husband: "It's wrong Martha. Horribly, horribly wrong. I cannot abide it anymore. I need to leave your father's employ. I need to get out of Charleston. Get away from this."

Wife: "Then go, Milton. Go. But you're going to go alone. Don't expect the children and me to go with you. To leave what we have here."

Husband: "Perhaps I shall, Martha. Perhaps I shall. It's wrong, Martha.

Horribly . . . horribly wrong. It's against God's Will.
"Perhaps I'll not even go into shipping.
"Perhaps I'll go to seminary instead.
"Study to become a preacher. A preacher and an abolitionist."

THE ASSASSIN

DeAndre Hawkins

Law School 1973 – 1976

FBI 1976 – 1978

Secret Service 1978 – 2022

Sunday, December 27, 6:27 a.m.

It was just after dawn and DeAndre Hawkins stood at the base of the Washington Monument gazing out across the reflecting pool toward the Lincoln Memorial. He was alone and it was early in the morning. The sun was just starting its slant across the rooftops of the still sleeping city.

The House of Representatives had yet to certify the electoral vote for the newly and duly elected President. That certification would occur in twelve days. The new President had won in an electoral college squeaker. And the incumbent president, who'd won by a similarly slim margin four years earlier, was upset about it. In fact, he had done everything in his power since the election to reverse the result; or, failing that, to cast doubt upon the election's legitimacy.

*

DeAndre was wide awake despite his lack of sleep the night before. He just couldn't get his mind to dismiss the news he received three days earlier at Walter Reed Hospital. The news his doctor told him. That he had pancreatic cancer. "But, DeAndre," the doctor said, "don't give up hope. There have been some very positive developments in treating this kind of cancer recently. Very positive and very encouraging. So, we're going to do all we can for you...use all of these new treatments in your case."

While DeAndre appreciated his doctor's encouragement, he didn't believe him. He knew a little bit about pancreatic cancer. He knew its survival rate was about seven percent. If that. And that those who got

Part One: Short Stories

it usually were gone in six to eight months. Jerry, his best friend from high school, survived nine months. *He always was a standout. Always did better than everyone else,* DeAndre remembered. *Turns out he was even above average for the survival rate of pancreatic cancer. But still, even he lost. He beat the average by over two months, but he still died. So the lesson is, once you get pancreatic cancer, you better start wrapping things up. Make a Will. Figure out where you want things to go. Shit like that,* he thought.

So, DeAndre didn't believe the good doctor's hope for recovery. And he could tell from the look on the doctor's face—particularly the flicker of disingenuousness in the doctor's eyes—that he didn't really believe what he was saying either. That he was just going through the standard "doctor-patient encouragement protocol" so DeAndre wouldn't lose heart and totally give up. While DeAndre knew that the best proven treatments generally produced the best results, a patient's positive attitude and spirit might also contribute to a favorable result. That sometimes made the difference between recovery and death. *The Christian Scientists may have a point,* he told himself. So, DeAndre charged himself to be positive. But deep down, he knew that, too, probably would be futile.

*

Driving back to D.C. from Walter Reed, DeAndre resolved he wouldn't tell anyone about the doctor's diagnosis. After all, he reasoned, who was there to tell? Who was there to confide in? His wife had left him sixteen years ago. And his daughter, now his only child, had sided with her mother. Neither of them had spoken to him for years. In fact, the last time he'd seen his daughter was when his mother, her grandmother, died. Even then, she just glanced at him across the aisle at the church then quickly turned away. And she scrupulously ignored him at the reception following the service.

DeAndre also decided not to tell anyone at the Secret Service about his condition. He was the oldest active-duty officer in the Service and quite the iconic figure there. He came by this status honestly and honorably in the line of duty. In 2003 when a protester broke free from the rope line as Vice President Chadwick was high fiving down the line, DeAndre sensed there was about to be trouble. So, when the protestor dropped his placard and started reaching under his jacket toward his left armpit, DeAndre immediately jumped in front of the Vice President. DeAndre took the protester's nine-millimeter in his right shoulder. But before the full impact of the slug knocked him backward, DeAndre fired a single shot from his Sig Sauer which felled the protester before he could get off a second and perhaps more accurate shot at the Veep.

DeAndre was an immediate hero in the media. The news channels played and replayed his actions taken during the assassination attempt. Even more importantly, he was extolled by the President, the Vice President, and the Service. Of all the accolades and tributes, however, the one from the Service—from his colleagues—was the one DeAndre valued the most. That was the one he treasured. The respect of his colleagues. Their admiration. Their veneration and respect. Praise and adulation from career politicians? Of what value was that? Everyone knows what they say is merely showy verisimilitude; nice words uttered for pragmatic or partisan purposes but devoid of any honesty, genuine belief or sincerity.

After he fully recovered from his gunshot wound, DeAndre returned to active duty and was assigned to the president's detail. He had guarded three since 2004, including the incumbent. This was the highest honor in the Secret Service. Guarding Number One. Guarding "Big Dog."

The president had personally asked that DeAndre be assigned to his security detail. The president, so DeAndre had heard, wanted an agent "who was experienced and had an intuitive eye for sensing danger. But even more importantly, one who'd proven he'd take a bullet; not just one who'd simply pledged to do so." So, DeAndre was now the president's main man, his detail leader. He'd demonstrated that he was willing to make the ultimate sacrifice if required. And the scar beneath his right shoulder blade proved it.

But now, seventeen years since the attempt on the Vice President's life and DeAndre's recovery from the gunshot wound, the challenge of being "the president's main man" was beginning to take its toll. DeAndre was in his late sixties, and it was becoming more and more difficult physically to do the job. To jog alongside the president's motorcade as he'd easily done in the past. So, DeAndre had to push himself harder and harder at the gym to keep up with the younger agents even minimally. *An old walrus must work harder to fend off the young buck challengers on the ice flow. So, you better just fuckin' outwork 'em,* DeAndre told himself.

Now, years later, having adhered to the goal of "outworking 'em," DeAndre, on his return from Walter Reed, resolved not to tell anybody anything about his illness. About any infirmity or weakness. *No fuckin' way are they gonna hear anything about it from me.*

Prior Years

DeAndre Hawkins was born in Hoboken, New Jersey in August 1951. He was an only child. His father was a chauffeur for a real estate mogul in New York and his mother worked as a dietitian in a high school cafeteria. Back then his name was Roosevelt Douglass Hawkins. For a variety of reasons—not the least of which was toning down the ideological implications of his name—he changed his name to DeAndre Hawkins during the summer between his second and third years in law school. And "DeAndre Hawkins" was what was printed on his law school diploma. Right before the Latin words "summa cum laude."

As a young Black law graduate—particularly one with a stellar academic record—DeAndre could have written his ticket with almost any of the prestigious law firms in New York, Boston, Philadelphia, or Washington. Wherever. Probably even Atlanta or Birmingham. Law firms throughout the country were tripping over themselves to show to the world—and mostly their clients—how progressive they were. And diversity was the most demonstrable badge of progressiveness.

He could have received well over $150K—big money for law school graduates in those days—if that's what he'd wanted. But that's not at all what he wanted. DeAndre wanted law enforcement. He was driven by that goal. So, despite his father's strong urgings to accept one of the "big money" offers and take advantage of the "opportunity provided by the changing times," DeAndre accepted a grunt level position with the FBI as a fingerprint analyst. Eventually, he hoped to work his way up the ladder in the Bureau so, as a leader in the organization, he could influence policy dealing with what he viewed as the decline in the country's moral values. Particularly the decline in values of the nation's leaders. Of those elected to high office. Of those who were supposed to represent the very best of the population. But his disdain wasn't limited to politicians. It applied CEOs, doctors, lawyers, academics and even to clergy who were corrupt or who abused their positions of power. To DeAndre, a career of fighting white collar crime, corruption and predatory sexual behavior was the highest calling of law enforcement. High, too, on his list was going after tax evaders, Ponzi scheme promoters and those in positions of power who exploited their elevated stations for illicit purposes. They were the real scum of the earth in his view. Those who preened their supposed ethics, integrity and morality were in reality just the opposite. Those were the most contemptable and reprehensible villains he wanted to bring down. To bring to justice.

He also had a strong sense of patriotism, a passion to serve the United States and protect what it stood for. To safeguard its institutions, its ideals, its Constitution. His father had fought for the country in World War II in one of the then-segregated Negro regiments and DeAndre was extremely proud of his father's service. He was also inspired by the stirrings of racial equality represented by the incipient integration of Blacks into society's mainstreams following the war. Examples set by Jackie Robinson and Rosa Parks. His country was finally starting to offer hope and promise for Blacks and DeAndre yearned to be part of the fulfillment of that hope and promise.

So rather than opting for a high-paying, associate position in a prestigious law firm, DeAndre accepted a job with the Bureau. But after nineteen months of analyzing fingerprints and performing other low-level tasks, he became frustrated. He felt his career was languishing. He wanted something more challenging and rewarding. Something more in line with his idealism and desire to serve and protect his country as his father had.

Thus, when he was approached by a recruiter for the Secret Service, he jumped at the opportunity.

Sunday, December 27, 6:38 a.m.

Weary of standing, DeAndre walked from the base of the Washington Monument to a nearby bench, lowered his head, and cupped his face in his hands. He thought back over his career of protecting the nation's top leaders and how that had been his life.

You protected those guys now for what . . . forty-four plus years . . . yeah that's right . . . at least forty-four . . . cabinet members . . . a chief-of-staff . . . the VP . . . took a bullet for Chadwick in 2003 . . . damn near died for that . . . got a medal for that and a ceremony to boot . . . big fuckin' deal . . . then the goddamn director goes and makes a fuckin' training video out of it . . . exploiting what you did . . . then the big promotion . . . seventeen years protecting THE MAN . . . every agent's goal . . . top of the profession . . . big fuckin' deal . . . just more respon-

sibility, but same fuckin' job . . . and what did you get for it . . . nothin' but a broken marriage . . . a messy divorce . . . your ex and your kid hating you . . . your ex's voice and her words echoing and reverberating in your head every waking hour and even in your dreams.

"How could you, DeAndre? How could you leave our little Reggie in Mattie's care alone? A five-year-old looking after a two-year-old? A toddler! You knew Mattie would want to go outside and play. A warm sunny day like that and you had to know she'd take Reggie outside with her. And you knew our house was on a busy street."

Over and over, you hear her say, "I trusted you'd take care of them while I was out, but then you left them alone. You left them to go and protect that goddamn senator from Mississippi. A racist bastard who hates Blacks no less. On your day off. When you said you wouldn't be called! When you assured me they wouldn't call you! But it's always the same . . . always your job . . . always your goddamn job. Job over family. Every time. We always come in second.

"And then I come home and see the ambulance and the cop cars, and I say 'Oh my God. They're in my driveway! Oh my God. Oh my God!'

"And now my little Reggie's gone and it's all your fault. My baby's gone. Hit by that truck when he toddled into the street. I hate you! I hate you! I want you gone too. I want you out of my life!"

Even your daughter hates you . . . won't forgive you. Sided with her mother after the divorce . . . won't even talk to you . . . won't even send you a Christmas card, for Christ's sake . . .

And what do you have to show for it . . . diddley squat set aside for your retirement . . . a shiny piece of metal hanging from a ribbon *that's not worth a goddamn dollar . . . probably not even the Smithsonian would take it . . . your daughter sure as hell won't . . . and your ex, Joannie? Forget about it . . . and what was it all for?*

Was it really smart takin' that bullet for Chadwick? Should you have stayed back? He was an asshole, and as it turned out, the country would have been better off without him. The country woulda stayed out of a war. And now you're riskin' your life every day for that racist, misogynistic grifter who's sittin' in the White House . . . what the fuck man . . . get real.

Then DeAndre's thoughts turned to the conversation he'd overheard when he stood outside the door to the Oval Office two days before Christmas. It was 9:30 a.m. and a server had just brought in Danish and coffee for the president, Wyatt Townsend; his Chief of Staff, Mack Sullivan; Buck Collins, a former Marine Corps General and now a Congressman from Ohio and Garrett Drummond, the Attorney General. The president had summoned them to the White House. He was furious because the Supreme Court had thrown out the Ohio appeal that its electoral vote—and that of three other states—should be declared void based on election fraud. A case, which if upheld, would have awarded the president a second term.

The server, in her haste to escape from the room highly charged by presidential wrath, hadn't fully closed the door between the anteroom and the Oval Office; and DeAndre, stationed in position to guard the Oval Office, could overhear everything that was being said inside.

DeAndre immediately recognized Collins' voice. "Look, Mr. President, I'm truly sorry about Ohio. I thought we had a pretty good

Part One: Short Stories

chance of throwing out my state's vote. We gave it a good shot anyway, got four votes at SCOTUS. If only those two turncoats, Bledsoe and Kraus you just appointed hadn't deserted the other conservatives."

"I know . . . I know . . . the ungrateful sons-a-bitches." President Townsend fumed. "You'd think there'd be loyalty . . . respect. That's what's in short supply these days. Fuckin' country's goin' to hell, I tell you," he said, "and it's my job to save it. Only I can save it. Restore it to what it should be. So no, Buck, it's not your fault. It was a very creative idea you came up with. Truly a novel argument. And you worked a veritable miracle getting the Ohio Attorney General to go along with it. To initiate the case in the first place. So, the fault's not yours. The fault's with those cocksuckers on the Supreme Court. Especially the ones I appointed to the Court. Those ungrateful bastards. Especially that cunt I rammed through with Leader McGregor's help just before the election."

DeAndre could sense the tension. He pictured Townsend pacing the perimeter of the room.

"But anyway," the president resumed, "tell me how things went in Arlington. At Party headquarters."

"Real good, Sir," Collins replied. "Real good. As you know, all of the major players were there. You know, Corey Westman, the lawyer from Texas who's come into the picture since election day . . ."

"Good, Westman's a good man." President Townsend opined.

Collins, continuing to suck up to the president, then added, "All of us were there and all your loyals: your Senior Advisor, Miller Stevens; the Campaign Chairman, Steve Scardino; the Press Secretary Melanie McDermot; Bill Walters from DOJ; Mack here; and, of course, me.

"Oh, and your buddy from 'Beautiful Sleep Pillows, Inc.' He was there too."

"What about you, Garrett?" the President asked. "Were you there?"

"No, Mr. President, I was not," Attorney General Drummond replied.

"Why not?" the president barked, "You're my Attorney General. Aren't you supposed to represent me?"

Drummond, choosing his words carefully replied, "No, Mr. President, as I've explained to you before, I represent the people, the country, and the Constitution. Not you personally, as an individual. Not even you as an individual president. I represent the office of the presidency, yes, and the executive branch, yes, but that's different. That's not any one single person even if that person happens to be you."

The president paused. He then muttered, "Mmmmm . . . I just don't get that. What's the fuckin' difference. You and your goddamned minute distinctions . . . well anyway, Buck, what did you guys come up with?"

"Quite a few things really. Things that we really feel good about. Stuff that just might work."

"Oh yeah, well then tell me about it." the president exclaimed impatiently. "Goddamn it, Buck, I don't have all day here. I've got a lot on my plate so tell me about it! Quit dancing around the flagpole!"

"Okay, okay. Probably the starting point was Westman's idea . . . you know, the one based on the electoral college certification process. It's quite ingenious. There's this statute called the Electoral College

Act that Congress enacted sometime after the Civil War. Westman says it's ambiguous in a potentially helpful way. He says it could be interpreted as giving the vice president authority to question and possibly throw out the electoral college votes of certain states if he determines there was error, foul play, or fraud. So, following that line of reasoning, here's what we can do. Once the vice president declares there was fraud shall we say in state X, a state of course that we lost . . . we certainly wouldn't want to do it in a state that we won . . . he then rejects the duly elected slate of electors from state X and we substitute a fake set of electors for X which we can easily concoct. Then we get our guys in state X to certify the election for X in accordance with the proper forms, submit them to Congress and the National Archives and presto you've got the electoral votes of state X. And if we do that in a sufficient number of states, you're now the president for a second term."

"Wow! I like it!" the president remarked excitedly.

"And," Collins continued, "we've already gone ahead with that part of the plan, Sir, subject to your approval, of course, and printed up the forms with the alternate slate of the phony . . . oh, I beg your pardon, I misspoke, with the 'proper, duly appointed, alternate electors' I meant to say. And those alternate electors have already signed and certified that they are the proper, duly appointed ones. So now all we have to do is submit the forms.

"And once we do that, the vice president does the rest. He'll declare there was fraud in those states and that the initial elector tallies were invalid and that the alternate slates are the proper ones. This will circumvent the Supreme Court's holding in the Ohio case; and when the original electoral college slates are thrown out, you'll be the winner and you'll be reelected. And that asshole Berens can go back to Delaware and start planning what would have been his presidential library."

"Mmmm . . . *s*ounds good." the president mused. "In theory at least. But will it work? Is it Constitutional? What do you think, Garrett?"

No goddamn way that's Constitutional! That's the most outrageous excretion of bullshit I've ever heard! Drummond thought. However, to appease President Townsend, what he said was, "Well, Sir, I have some doubts about its constitutionality, but I'll check into it."

"Well, Garrett, your man Walters from DOJ, he said it had merit and was a plausible reading of the statute." Collins added.

"I'll check into it." Drummond replied. "I'll talk with Walters about it. It's creative, I'll give you that."

The President sneered, "Don't give me that 'I'll check into it,' bullshit dodge, Garrett. I'm hearing too much of that from you these days. Those wishy-washy, namby-pamby, indecisive positions you keep giving me. I want good, solid, positive answers. The right answers that back up what I say the law is or what it should be. Anyway Buck, what did Westman have to say about the constitutionality?"

"He says it's constitutional. Arguable anyway. He says it's never been tested before, but he says there's something in the 1887 legislative history . . . in the preamble to the statute, and some helpful language in the Federalist Papers . . . that tends to support it and that we should give it a shot. Depends upon Vice President Spencer to a large extent."

"That lap dog. That spaniel. Jesus, I hate to rely on him," the president complained. "He's nothing but a placebo, if you ask me."

"Yeah, but under the constitution, he's the one who counts the Electoral College votes and certifies 'em. So, he's the one we've got to rely upon."

"That spineless wimp," the president grumbled. "Remember the time when he was sitting next to me at some conference. I'm at the head of the table and he's to my right, and I pick up my soda can and put it on the floor and then he does the same thing! Jesus Christ, what a copycat little toady! God, I hate to have to count on him to do anything that requires backbone!"

"I know, Chief, but he's the one whose gotta do it," Sullivan remarked.

"Okay, okay. Maybe the wimp will come through for me for once. So what do you think, Garrett?"

"Well, Sir, to be candid, I have my doubts." Drummond replied. "The Veep's job has always been just ceremonial . . . ministerial . . . just to count the votes from the states and then to certify them . . ."

"God damnit, Garrett, there you go again. I told you not to give me one of your mushy, mealy-mouthed fucking answers. I want straightforward answers and a tough plan of action. And this sounds like a good one. I think Westman's a good man . . . a damn good lawyer. I like his style. No namby-pamby bullshit like I get all the time from DOJ and from you. Westman's got . . . say . . . wait a minute. Hold on here. He graduated from Harvard Law School, didn't he Mack?"

"Yes, Sir. That's right."

"That's what I thought. Harvard. And where'd you go to law school, Garrett?"

"I went to Marbury State, Sir."

The president turned and glared at his attorney general, "I thought so! Anyway, this is a serious matter, so I need a serious answer and a serious plan."

Drummond lowered his head and thought, *Damn right, this is a serious matter and I can't let this turn into a serious plan.*

"So, anyway Buck," the president resumed, "you tell Westman that I like his reasoning and that he should develop it further. I'll make him Special Counsel on this, so we won't have to go through DOJ and Garrett, here."

Drummond turned his head, mumbled, and whispered to the wall, "This guy's got too many snake-oil salesmen giving him bad advice and wild-ass, outrageous arguments as to what the vice president can do! This is fucking insanity!" He didn't realize how close he was to the anteroom; and DeAndre, being close by, heard every word the AG muttered.

"Okay then, let's move on that," the president concluded. Then, continuing, he said, "Buck, you said there were a couple of other things. What else did you guys come up with?"

"Lots of good stuff, Mr. President. It's quite comprehensive too. I'll let Mack tell you about that, Sir. He's more facile in strategy aspects than I am."

"Thanks, Buck." Sullivan began. "Here's what else the guys at Arlington came up with . . . strategy wise, that is. It's multifaceted, Mr. President, but it all starts with the allegation—false of course—that there was massive election fraud and . . ."

The president, turning red, shouted, "What the fuck, Mack! Are you turning on me? What do you mean that 'election fraud' is false?

Part One: Short Stories

What the fuck do you mean that it wasn't 'massive'? Of course, there was election fraud! And, of course it was 'massive!' It was unprecedented, monumental, massive fraud! Fraud on a scale never seen in the history of this country . . . in the history of the world, even! There had to be! How else could I have lost if there wasn't massive fraud? I mean . . . I mean . . . I'm ME! And I'm not a loser. No way, not me. I'm no loser! So there must have been fraud. Massive fraud, I tell you. There was no way that shrivel dick, sleepy little asshole Berens . . . could'a beaten me if there wasn't fraud. Ballots from Pennsylvania dumped in a creek. Georgia, that can't count straight. Arizona, all those sleazy bastards in Maricopa County. I mean everyone knows there was bamboo in the ballots and that caused the ballots to switch from Townsend to Berens. Can't you fucking see that! Even you, Garrett, don't you know that bamboo can do that? Jesus Christ, I remember that from my high school science class.

"There's no fucking way I could'a lost. Fraud! Fraud! I tell you! Massive fucking fraud! Come on, Mack, get with it!"

Sullivan, cowed and intimidated by the president's outburst, warily and cautiously replied, "Okay, okay, Chief. Here's what the Arlington group decided. The over-arching strategy that is. It starts with multiple allegations of fraud. Fraud in multiple states. Then we start lawsuits; not just in Ohio, but in Arizona, Pennsylvania, Michigan, and Wisconsin . . . states that Berens supposedly won. Even states where you won, like Texas, for example, just to show that we're not cherry-picking . . . you know, a subterfuge to throw off the media…sew some doubt in those states 'cause we know we'll win anyway in a recount. And we hammer home the idea that the election was corrupt.

That there was election fraud. Fraud on such a massive, monumental scale that has never happened before."

"That's more like it," the president interrupted. "Like I just said. Massive, unprecedented fraud. Fraud, the likes of which has never before been seen in this country before. In the entire history of the world, for that matter. Unprecedented, massive fucking fraud."

"So anyway, Mr. President," Sullivan continued, "we bolster our case with incidents like the Pennsylvania ballot destruction situation. And there are other theories . . . foreign intervention . . . the Russians hacking once again . . . ballot alteration by computerized voting machines made in Venezuela . . . bamboo in Arizona's ballots by the Chinese like you said . . . all kinds of bad shit. All of it bullshit, of course. But, hey, if it works, who cares. We win. You win.

"Oh, and there's more thing. One more thing that's really got potential and is really powerful. We put pressure on the states. On their legislatures and their secretaries of state, whoever does their election certification. We get them to do recounts, to challenge the vote totals, and switch the votes around. Not, of course, in states where you legitimately won. Just in those states where you came in a close second."

"Mmmm . . . I see," the president responded. "I suppose I could call some state governors or secretaries of state . . . whoever is in charge of the counting and ask 'em to see if they could find some more votes for me."

"Yeah, that might be helpful, Sir," Sullivan replied. "Hopefully, they'd be willing to do that. And if you ask them personally . . . with the full weight of your office behind the ask . . . it just might work."

Jesus Christ, this shit is getting out of hand!" Drummond thought. *Way fucking out of hand.*

"But hang on a minute here." the president cautioned, "if we toss out the election results for the presidency, won't that knock out some of the down ballot victories for our guys? For Senate, for Congressional seats, for state office results?"

Sullivan hesitated, "Well . . . ahhhh . . . well I guess we'd have to say that the fraud only related to the top of the ballot. To the presidential vote. Not to the down ballot positions like the Senate, the House of Representatives, and state offices. You know, like computer hackers can do anything. Like they just manipulated the top ballot position."

Sullivan then paused, letting this theory sink in. When no one challenged it or added to it, he went on. "Of course, after things cool down a bit. Next year when the state legislatures return to session, we can gerrymander the shit out of the state congressional districts, so we never lose control of the House of Representatives again. And, oh yeah, we get the states that are deep red to pass statutes authorizing their legislatures to change the election results if for some reason we do lose an election . . . you know, reverse the vote of the people . . . the ignorant masses that never should'a been allowed to vote in the first place."

Drummond had heard enough at this point and felt emboldened enough to speak out. "Jesus, Mack, you can't be serious! That's preposterous! Outrageous! That would destroy our democracy. Not to mention be a flagrant violation of the Constitution!"

"Yeah, so what? We'd be the winners, wouldn't we?" the president growled. "We'd be in control, wouldn't we? We'd stay in power, wouldn't we?"

Drummond just shook his head in disbelief.

"Anyway, Sir," Sullivan resumed, trying to defuse matters. "That's the overall picture of what we came up with at Arlington. There may be some kinks and flaws that need to be worked out. And we'll have to put a gloss on some of it, of course, but those are the main points we came up with."

"That's all well and good, Mack," the president continued, "but getting the states to pass new laws gerrymandering Congressional Districts and enabling state legislatures to reverse elections when they don't like the results, that's all in the future and the future doesn't concern me. That's not what we need for THIS election. I don't give a shit about future elections," the president asserted emphatically. "That's not going to help me now! I want stuff that's gonna help me now! This election was stolen from me, and I want it reversed."

Collins, suddenly inspired by a new and different strategy, interrupted the president's rant, "Wait a minute! Hold on! What you just said, Mr. President...what you just said has given me a great idea. A great slogan. You just said the election was stolen from you. We oughta be able to make that into a nice catchy slogan...something that would really catch on...that people could rally around...like 'Stop the Stolen election!' No, that's too long. It's gotta be shorter than that. I know . . . 'Stop the Steal'. That's short and catchy and you could use that as a rallying cry."

"Mmm . . . '*Stop the Steal*,' the president repeated. "I like it. It's got a nice ring to it. I definitely could use that.

"Great idea, Buck! Great idea! 'Stop the Steal!' I love it. What do you think, Mack?"

"Sounds good to me, Chief. Kinda rolls off the tongue. Yeah, 'Stop the Steal'! I think that would make a great bumper sticker," Mack Sullivan concluded.

"But there's more, Mr. President, more that we can do," Collins continued. "Extra stuff to nail down the election reversal and keep you in office. 'Cuz it's always better to have more ammunition, more fire power than you think you'll need. The more fire power the better, I always said to my colonels. So, here's some other shit we can do to change things, so we'll prevail. If the audits of the election results don't come out the way we want and if the state legislatures don't reverse the bad results, then we can have you seize the voting machines and . . ."

"Wait a minute, how am I going to do that?" the president demanded.

"Simple. You're the president. You can issue Executive Orders."

"I know that, but on what basis?"

"It's a federal election. There were irregularities, allegations of massive voter fraud. Foreign nation interference. We—the federal government that is—need to intervene to be certain the integrity of our election is preserved."

Drummond muttered under his breath. "Yeah, 'preserve the integrity of our election' by illegally reversing the election! What a crock of shit! 'Integrity' becomes falsehood. Just the opposite. Everything is turned upside down. This is fucking Orwellian! This is fucking bullshit! These guys are out of their fucking minds! What the fuck should I do?"

"But who?" asked the president. "Who am I going to get to seize the voting machines? Not the DOJ. The FBI? They probably won't do it. And Federal Marshalls aren't equipped to do it."

"Well, we think because it's a federal matter pertaining to national security that the Department of Homeland Security can do it." Sullivan said. "And if not them, the National Guard. And once we get a hold of the voting machines . . . well, do I have to elaborate? I think you can figure out how we'd deal with that.

"And if none of that works, we go to the streets. We have protests. Here in Washington and in cities and towns across the country. Create mayhem. Disorder. Rioting. You name it. Maybe we can even have your faithful rebels storm state capitals, arrest some state secretaries of state, maybe even some state governors. Arrest them at night in their homes!"

At this, Drummond felt that he had to speak out. That he couldn't hold back. "Wait! Wait, just a goddamn minute! Did I hear you correctly, Mack? Did I hear you say storm the state capitols? Arrest state governors? That's totalitarianism! That's dictatorship! That's like what happens in banana republics!"

Sullivan persisted, "You heard me right, Garrett. Storm state capitols, arrest state governors. Arrest anybody that gets in our way. That's what I said and that's what I meant!"

Totally frustrated and at wits end, Drummond raised his voice, "Are you out of your fucking mind? I can't imagine such a thing! I can't imagine that the Chief of Staff of the United States of America, the primary advisor to the president, his chief protector and facilitator . . . would even think of such a thing! Let alone say it out loud and advocate it to the president. In the fucking Oval Office no less! This is madness! This is shocking! It's incomprehensible."

Part One: Short Stories

"Bullshit! Bullshit, Garrett!" argued Sullivan, "Where the fuck have you been the last hour? Haven't you heard anything we've been talking about? The election has been sto—"

"You're fucking wrong! The election wasn't stolen. And you fucking know it! There's no plausible evidence of massive fraud or of a stolen election. All you've got is a theory in search of facts…evidence to back it up. You're just a candy-assed, sycophant coddling and sucking up to the president's fantasy and you fucking know it!" the Attorney General shouted.

The president interrupted. "Hold on! Hold on there, Garrett! Let Mack proceed, for Christ's sake. For MY sake really!"

To that, Drummond muttered, barely audibly, but loud enough so that DeAndre could overhear, "Yeah, for Christ's sake . . . that's even more bullshit. It's not for Christ's sake, it's for YOUR sake. It's been clear from the beginning you think you're equivalent of Christ. Some messianic, self-anointed deity. Well, you know what? Someone's got to nail you to a fucking cross or we're all gonna go down," Drummond, muttered barely audibly, but loud enough so that DeAndre could overhear.

"So go ahead, Mack, tell me more," the president commanded.

"Okay, okay. I will if Garrett here will shut the fuck up and let me proceed. Here's the ultimate plan: Plan C or Plan D, or whatever if we need it since we gotta be sure we don't fail. It's quite simple. We have a huge rally here in Washington on January 6th, the day that Congress is supposed to have the electoral college count . . . and you declare that the election was rigged, that there was fraud of an unprecedented, massive scale, and the fuckin' socialists are gonna take over the country unless we're strong and we fight. Then you say to your faithful followers who are there . . . particularly to the militias we've been in contact with, the Proud Boys, the Oath Keepers, and the First Amendment Praetorians . . . you know, the militia groups I told you about last week, you say to them 'you patriots have gotta protest. You've gotta go down to the Capitol and make your voices heard.' But you don't explicitly say 'storm the Capitol'. That could be deemed as inciting a riot or breaking the law. So, you don't say anything like that. We have to protect you from those bastards on the Judiciary Committee, as well as the communist, leftist press. We gotta give you cover, so to speak . . . right, Mr. President?"

The President squared his shoulders. "Yep. I'm with you one hundred percent. So go on Mack."

Sullivan then continued, "So anyway, the leaders of those militia groups will know what you mean 'cuz I will have talked with them beforehand. And you say you'll be with them. But you won't, of course, because that could get you into real trouble if you did. Impeachment-kind of trouble. So, those radicals will then storm the Capitol during the joint session of Congress before that wimp of a vice president starts calling the roll of the states . . . and the whole fucking proceeding is disrupted, and chaos ensues and there is no electoral count. No certification of the election."

The president sat back, thumbed his double chin, and mulled over what he'd just heard and was still processing. Then after nodding his head affirmatively, he said, "So, all I've gotta do is give the signal to the Proud Boys, Oath Keepers, and the First Amendment Praetorians to storm the Capital Building on the 6th and they'll proceed like you said?"

"Yep."

"And that'll be enough to stop the Congress from counting the electoral ballots?"

"Yep. The leaders of those groups have assured me they've got over ten thousand dedicated patriots who will show up with guns and battering rams and Tasers. And they'll be wearing camouflage uniforms and carrying zip-ties to restrain those Democrap bastards. Those traitors. And they'll also have crowbars and baseball bats. Even Confederate flags. And by the time you rev 'em up, Mr. President, they'll be itching to storm the chambers where the House and the Senate will be meeting and with any luck they'll seize that vice president son-of-a-bitch . . . and if they can catch that slut Speaker of the House, Perrone, they'll lynch 'em both. One of the Oath Keepers has even built a gallows replete with a noose he'll be bringing to the rally.

"So anyway, they'll create chaos and disorder sufficient so that you could declare martial law, prevent the electoral college certification, and postpone the inauguration of Berens 'cuz you'd still be in office.

"And Westman says there's even another federal statute that's helpful . . . that authorizes you to do this. It's called the Insurrection Act of 1807. Westman says if there's an insurrection or a rebellion against the country, the president's got the authority to deploy the military anywhere in the United States to quell the uprising."

The president grinned and rubbed his hands together. "Great! I love it! What do you think Garrett? Sounds to me like it's perfect!

Gives me the authority to order up the troops. And that's something I've always wanted to do anyway."

Drummond tried to check himself, but he had reached his limit and couldn't hold back any longer. "Mr. President!" he exclaimed, raising his voice and nearly shouting, "Mr. President, this is bullshit! Pure, unadulterated bullshit! You can't create an insurrection in order to activate the Insurrection Act. That's absurd! No court in the land would uphold that!"

"Why not? Sounds pretty good to me. Doesn't matter what caused it. If there's an insurrection and I've got the authority to call out the military to stop it! Why can't I?"

"Because you can't Mr. President, you simply can't. You can't be like the arsonist who sets the fire and then gets the 'Hero of the Year' award for calling the fire department to put it out!"

The president, disgusted with his attorney general turned to his chief of staff and said, "Forget about him, Mack. What you're telling me sounds beautiful to me . . . plain fucking beautiful. So, tell me more."

"Okay. Sure. There is more thing we came up with. Once the troops put down the rebellion, you declare there'll be a new election. And this time we'll be in full control of the election and the ballot boxes and voting machines because you'll decree that the states can't be trusted on account of the state of martial law. And I don't have to tell you about how THAT election will come out.

"Then," Mack Sullivan, pleased that his suggestion had been so well received, decided to add one more juicy little tidbit, "and you know what might be frosting on the cake? We blame it all on Antifa. We say that it wasn't our supporters who rioted; it was the radical, leftist Antifas, the leftist, socialist Democrats that did it. We say they're the ones who infiltrated the crowd and stirred 'em up. Not our people. And we'll be blameless. Lily white, so to speak. And we can create some false evidence to that effect . . . install some plants . . . so to speak."

The President beamed, "Perfect! Brilliant, Mack! Fox News will love it . . . they'll eat it up.

"Now remember, like I've said dozens of times before, none of this is to be in writing. No memos. No emails. No hard evidence of any kind. And no 'contemporaneous memos' stuck under your blotters or filed away in your underwear drawer. And for my part, no memos or records I've got to tear up and flush down the toilet, so they won't go into the National Archives."

"Got it, Chief. Got it. No memos. Nothing in writing. No hard evidence of any sort," Collins replied.

Sullivan concurred, "Yes sir. Duly noted. I'll make sure it doesn't happen. Oh, and Sir, one more thing . . ."

"Yeah, what's that?"

"I suggest you keep on repeating, over and over, every chance you get, that the election was stolen from you. You know, like Goebbels said: 'If you say something loud enough and often enough . . . even if it's a lie . . . people will believe it.' It worked for Hitler and the Nazis, and it can work for us as well."

The president squared his shoulders, "You know, you're absolutely right. I'll do it. Anything else boys?"

The president's men looked at each other. No one spoke.

"Okay then, let's take a break for lunch and come back in an hour to discuss where we go from here," the president concluded.

Buck Collins and Mack Sullivan then got up and proceeded out of the room.

As the others departed, Attorney General Drummond rose, walked slowly, deliberately toward the president, paused and then said, "I resign, Mr. President. It's been my honor to have served you, Mr. President, but now's the time for me to step down. I'll have my letter of resignation delivered to you in the morning. And I think I'll skip the meeting you're going to have after lunch today."

*

After lunch, as the three of them resumed their respective positions in the oval office, the president sitting behind The Resolute desk, his Chief of Staff, Mack Sullivan, and Buck Collins seated on the sofas perpendicular to The Resolute desk. The president folded his arms across his ample stomach and began, "Well boys, I have a positive announcement. That no good attorney general of mine resigned just before we broke for lunch and that frees me up to appoint someone more loyal and shall we say, 'more cooperative' with respect to the position we've adopted. On an acting basis, of course, so I don't have to go through the charade of an official confirmation proceeding in the Senate. And I know just whom I'll appoint . . . Westman.

"Anyway, Drummond's resignation frees us up to proceed without any speed bumps he'd likely present."

Part One: Short Stories

"Good," Buck Collins said.

"That's great, Mr. President," his chief-of-staff, Mack Sullivan added.

"So anyway, boys, now that we've gotten the AG out of the way, where do we go from here? How do we put all these plans into motion? Where and when do we start? We're gonna have to lay the groundwork if we're gonna have a big, humongous rally in DC. To set the table, so to speak. We can't just have this one big, colossal rally occur out of the blue. We've got to have some prelims…some preparatory events, don't you think? But what? Where? When?"

DeAndre Hawkins, having resumed his post outside the doorway, leaned toward the crack in the partially open door.

Mack Sullivan and Buck Collins just looked at one another in silence. They hadn't thought about the need to have a preliminary event. An event that would "lay the groundwork" or "set the table" for a big rally in DC as the president now directed. And they were momentarily stumped. Finally, General Buck Collins spoke up, "Here's an idea for you, Mr. President. What about Cleveland? That's where we had the Party's convention in 2016, as you'll recall. And we've got some pretty good contacts there . . . some pretty good infrastructure, if you will. So, I'm sure I could set something up there right after the first of the year. Right downtown in Public Square."

"Brilliant, Buck. Brilliant. I love it. Public Square's a big open area as I recall. It would hold a big crowd. And you're right, we've got some real good contacts there. At least at the state level. And good 'infrastructure' as you say, so we should be able to get something set up really quick. And it's midwestern too. That's a plus. I don't want to launch 'Stop the Steal' on either one of the leftist, socialist coasts.

"So, Cleveland it will be. I know exactly what I'll say. I'll deliver the fieriest, most impassioned speech I've ever given. I'll get the crowd all riled up and the folks who aren't there will wish they had been after they've heard what I've said on TV. I'll tell my people that the election was the greatest crime in American history . . . an atrocity which has no peer. Even worse than slavery and that they've got to rectify it. That they've got to be patriots. I'll tell them it's their civic duty to come to Washington on the 6th to 'Stop the Steal'.

"And if they do show up in D.C. on the 6th in sufficient numbers and with sufficient energy, maybe that wimp Spencer will somehow have the balls to decertify the vote and reverse the electoral college results."

Collins smiled, "That sounds terrific, Mr. President. That'll set the stage real nice for the rally in DC on the 6th."

The president, hopeful and determined, then said, "Okay then. Let's get the ball rolling. I want results. I want this done. You guys have the big picture, now let's do it.

"Buck, you set it up Cleveland. Do whatever it takes. Whatever it costs and leave the rest to me."

The meeting was over. The president got up from the Resolute Desk and headed toward the anteroom. Mack Sullivan and Buck Collins rose from the sofas, waited respectfully for the president to pass, then headed toward the main exit of the Oval Office.

*

Part One: Short Stories

For several seconds, Deandre Hawkins just stood inside the anteroom absorbing what he'd heard. He was stunned. Shocked. Paralyzed and couldn't move. He couldn't believe what he'd just heard. The president of the United States of America and his chief advisors planning the overthrow of the government, planning a coup against the country they had taken oaths to preserve and protect. For the president, his oath was taken with his right hand raised and his left placed upon a Bible. The Lincoln Bible, no less.

Then, as he heard the president's footsteps heading toward the anteroom, DeAndre quickly retreated a few steps further back from the door so the president wouldn't think he'd overheard what had been said. When the president entered the anteroom, DeAndre stiffened to attention and greeted the president with the same formal salute he'd always given to the commander-in-chief. At least he thought it was the same.

At that moment, Mack Sullivan glanced back toward the anteroom as the president left the Oval Office. He saw DeAndre snap to attention and salute the president as he had seen him do countless times in the past. But he wasn't so sure DeAndre's salute was the same as those he'd observed before. There was a slight hesitation, a slight dipping of DeAndre's eyes that made him wonder. *That Secret Service guy . . . what's his name . . . I should know his name . . . he's the Chief's main man . . . did he overhear what we were talking about? Was that door completely shut when the Pres, Buck, and I were talking just now? And what if he overheard what we discussed before lunch when Garrett was with us? Jesus, Mary, Mother of God, I sure hope the fuck he didn't overhear any of those conversations. And we wonder how leaks from this fucking place occur. Jesus, fucking Christ!*

General Buck Collins didn't notice DeAndre at all. He simply strode purposefully with parade-ground steps toward the main exit of the Oval Office.

Neither did the president notice any change in DeAndre's demeanor. He simply walked purposefully past DeAndre into the anteroom. To him, DeAndre was as inanimate as a marble statue.

Sunday, December 27, 6:52 a.m.

DeAndre Hawkins lifted his head from his hands and gazed across the Reflecting Pool toward the Lincoln Memorial once again. *Jesus fucking Christ . . . I protect this guy and I know what he thinks, what he's about to do and what he's capable of . . . and I know there's no one around him to stop him . . . and now me with my cancer . . . what the fuck am I doing guarding this fucker . . . this son-of-a-bitch . . . this son-of-a-bitch who's threatening to destroy our democracy . . . imperiling our Constitution . . . the one person whose primary duty it is to preserve and protect the Constitution is the very one who's trying to destroy it . . . to ride roughshod over it. Jesus fucking Christ, Andre, why the fuck are you protecting him when he's the biggest threat to our democracy, to our rule of law? You're protecting the fucker who's plotting to violate his constitutional duty to protect the democracy that you've taken an oath to protect? What the fuck, man? This is all fucked up . . . it's all upside down! What the fuck are you doing?*

DeAndre didn't finish his thoughts. Instead, he abruptly stood up, shook his head, and then pressed his hands hard against his temples. He paced back and forth around the Washington Monument then strolled into the city itself. He had no particular destination in mind. He just walked and continued thinking.

After a few blocks, DeAndre stopped in front of St. John's Church where the president, the Attorney General, and the Chairman of the Joint Chiefs had led a march a month earlier. It was where, after using tear gas and helicopters, low and hovering, with gale-force torrents of crushing winds, the military police had dispersed a peaceful protest; where the president had held up a Bible to demonstrate the purported righteousness of his cause; where, as DeAndre recalled with a smirk, the president, unintentionally, but symbolically, held the Bible upside down. *Dumb bastard, he can't even hold a Bible right!*

DeAndre stopped in front of the church staring at its sign welcoming the faithful to attend the service that would begin in a couple of hours.

A scrap of paper diverted him. It was a hot dog wrapper that blew across the pavement, impaling itself on a leafless, broken twig that had fallen to the sidewalk. DeAndre bent down, picked up the wrapper and deposited it in a nearby trash receptacle. Then he went back, picked up the twig and threw it into the trash receptacle as well.

Still deep in thought, he walked back to the bench beside the Washington Monument where he'd previously been sitting. He sat down again staring straight ahead—again in the direction of Lincoln—but not really seeing anything. He remained deep in thought. *He's got-*

ta go. *The fucker's planning a goddammed coup for Christ's sake. A fuckin' coup! Here in America. A coup! Who'd ever have believed it? And it's the fuckin' president who is planning it! Jesus fucking Christ! And I protect this bastard?*

This is the son-of-a-bitch who's plotting what would be the worst event in American history . . . arguably worse than Pearl Harbor and certainly worse than 9-11 . . . those were bad, horrific acts . . . but overthrowing the government by the leader of the government! By the president himself! Jesus fucking Christ, this is treason at the highest level . . . what can be worse? And it's the fucking president who's planning and leading it!

And he's the person you took an oath to protect . . . an oath to your country and to God, for Christ's sake. How can you go against that? Yeah, but to protect him so he can destroy the country . . . our rule of law, our democracy . . . shit no, that ain't right . . . your basic duty is to the Constitution and to the country . . . not to one man.

DeAndre paused, looked up and stared long and hard off in the distance. Off to the figure beyond the Reflecting Pool. Off to the statue of Abraham Lincoln. Then he thought: *This man you're supposed to protect, he's the one who's got the duty to safeguard the Constitution. But what if the fucker doesn't do what he's supposed to do? What if he in fact does the opposite of what he's supposed to do? What are you supposed to do then? Protect the fucker who's trying to destroy the Constitution and the country he's supposed to protect? Shit, man! That ain't fuckin' right! He's gotta go. He's simply fuckin' gotta go. Impeachment didn't work. Everyone who's honest knows that what he did was wrong . . . that the son-of-a-bitch was guilty of doing what he was accused of and impeached for . . . that it was wrong . . . that he should have been convicted . . . but the fuckin', spineless sycophants in the Senate didn't have the balls to convict the son-of-a-bitch. The people fired him with the election last November, but now the fucker's trying to steal the election from them . . . and he's the one saying 'Stop the Steal' when he's the one who's plotting the steal . . . how the fuck more cynical can you get than that! He's the one who's doing the stealing, not those who he's accusing. And there's no one to stop the bastard. Not the Senate, not the Attorney General . . . and his lackey Chief of Staff and that fuckin' war-mongering General . . . they aren't gonna do anything to stop him. They're all in cahoots, the fuckers. So, who's gonna do somethin' about it, DeAndre? Who? Who's gonna save the Constitution and our democracy? Are the Brits gonna cross the ocean once again . . . this time to save us from ourselves? Is Canada gonna come down across the border to rescue us? Who, DeAndre, who?*

And you, you dumb fuckin' son-of-a-bitch . . . what the fuck have you done with your fuckin' life . . . a busted marriage . . . your own kid won't speak to you . . . won't even glance across the aisle of a church to look at you. You've spent more than forty years trying to protect our government's leaders and now this fuckin' president is threatening to destroy the very country he took an oath to protect, and you've taken an oath to protect him . . . and nobody's gonna do anything about it 'cuz nobody knows what he's planning to do. And in a few days, there's gonna be an insurrection that could easily lead to an authoritarian regime . . . an authoritarian regime right here in America, for Christ's sake . . . and you're sittin' here on your fat ass whining about it but not doin' anything about it.

And besides all of that, you're dying of cancer . . . and what the fuck have you ever really done with your life? Saved the life of a vice-president . . . yeah, big fuckin' deal...and so you got a medal for that...a pat on the back and a "way to go DeAndre" . . . big fuckin' deal . . . but this, this really is a big fuckin' deal. And only you know about it and nobody else does. And there's nobody in a position to prevent what you know is gonna happen from happening in just a few days except you DeAndre. Except you!

So, what the fuck, DeAndre. What the fuck are you gonna do about it . . . you . . . you, little Black boy DeAndre? What the fuck are you gonna do about it? Are you simply gonna go with the flow? Ride along with this fucker because you took an oath to protect him when now he's revealed he's plotting to do the unthinkable? What the fuck, DeAndre, others have faced the same dilemma you're facing . . . taken a sworn oath to some son-of-a bitch who turns out to be a fuckin' monster and they did the right thing . . . or at least they tried to. Who was that Nazi officer? Von something or other who tried to assassinate Hitler, I think it was. Yeah, Von something or other . . . I'll think of his name . . . it'll come to me. But I remember it was 'Von' and he took this solemn oath to protect Hitler . . . like all the Nazi officers . . . and he wrestled with himself about that oath. He was a Christian and some of the theologians of his church were preachin' that Hitler was the Antichrist and that Christians had a moral duty to eliminate the Antichrist. And that's what this 'Von' officer tried to do . . . follow his moral duty . . . what his church leader said was his higher duty, but shit, man, your case is different, it's—no, no, you're wrong, DeAndre, you Black motherfuck-

er—*you're just tryin' ta go back to bein' a servile, Black lackey motherfucker, when you know in your heart what your fuckin' duty is. You know in your heart that the fucker you've sworn to protect is nothin' but a monster—a would-be tyrant and the second coming of the Antichrist.*

Then DeAndre looked up at the tall obelisk he was sitting next to. He noticed that the sun had fully risen, and that the obelisk was now casting a shadow. A long shadow pointing toward the Reflecting Pool and beyond. Pointing toward the Lincoln Memorial.

Abraham Lincoln. Yeah, he's the one. He had the fortitude, the courage, and the strength of character to save the nation.

What about you, DeAndre?

What about you, you Black motherfucker?

Do you have the guts, the balls, to do the right thing, to do what you know you should do?

Sunday, December 27, 11:36 p.m.
After the Last Sunday Night NFL Game for the Regular Season Concluded

DeAndre sat by himself in the booth at O'Shaughnessy's Pub. Except for a couple of bathroom visits, he'd been sitting there since the 1:00 game. He'd had lunch, followed by a bowl of chili at 4:30 and dinner at 7:30. Crab cakes and succotash. And of course, a few beers.

But now, now he was twirling a scotch—a Johnnie Black—and making notes. Occasionally, he looked up staring off into a space high above the bottles on the top shelf behind the bar. Staring off and thinking.

*

Von Stauffenberg! Yeah, that's it. Von Stauffenberg. He's the one that tried to assassinate Hitler 'cuz he knew the guy was a malevolent megalomaniac . . . the Antichrist . . . evil incarnate who was destroying his country . . . destroying Europe, for Christ's sake . . . that he was an abomination and that he had to go. So, despite his oath of loyalty to the fucker, he decided to kill him. He didn't succeed, but he tried. And he's one of the few fuckin' Nazi officers that are now regarded as heroes.

So, what's it gonna be, DeAndre? Are you gonna step up? Are you gonna be a fuckin' hero for your country again? Like 2003? Be a hero like Von Stauffenberg, even if nobody knows about it?

*

Twenty more minutes went by, and DeAndre just sat there twirling his now lukewarm scotch. *So how the fuck are you gonna do it, DeAndre? How the fuck are you fuckin' gonna do it?*

*

What about at one of his rallies? Like the one he's gonna have in Cleveland? He usually likes to relieve himself before he goes on stage . . . being the leader of the detail, I could go into the john ahead of him . . . clear everybody else out, then go back in. We'd be alone and I could do him when he's in one of the stalls because he doesn't like to stand at one of the urinals . . . he's probably afraid he'll dribble or something, being an old guy. And I could then run out and say someone

Part One: Short Stories

was in there that I didn't shoo out . . . waiting for him and who shot him . . . and I shot back at him but missed . . . but I think he might have hit the president . . . there'd be lots of commotion . . . pandemonium . . . and the other Secret Service guys and the crowd would rush in . . . it'd be chaotic . . . and I could say later on that they guy who shot him got away in all of the commotion. Then I could slip away and get the hell outta there . . . maybe get to Kettle Creek or perhaps the north woods in Michigan . . . I don't know...plenty of places . . . Idaho . . . Montana . . . No, no, that would never work . . . I'd probably get caught leaving the john . . . and if not, and they'd find the slug that killed the president and they'd know it came from my piece, so I'd have to have another gun, or else they'd know it was me . . . What about carrying an extra gun? No, I'd somehow have to get rid of it. Besides they'd want to question me extensively and I couldn't just slip away because otherwise they'd figure it was me because I'd have disappeared . . . I don't want anyone to know it was me . . . it would ruin my reputation . . . I'd be another John Wilkes Booth . . . and I don't want that . . . my life's been fucked up enough as it is . . . I don't need to fuck it up even more by bein' labeled a fuckin assassin for all time . . . especially since I'd be the one who was supposed to protect him. And besides all of that if I killed him, I'd make him a martyr and I'd be a heinous villain and I sure as hell don't want that . . . my life's been fucked up enough as it is . . . but I've still got my medal from 2003 for saving Chadwick's life . . . still got that, for Christ's sake . . . I've still got my rep.

*

DeAndre put down his scotch. Stared up past the bar again. Harder. Then he got up, took a last swig of his scotch, put the empty glass back down on the table and started for the door.

"Fuck it," he said quietly to himself, "See ya next week, Willie."

"You got it, DeAndre. Have a nice night. Great night for your Browns."

"Yeah, never thought they'd come back after they got down by ten . . . against the Steelers, no less."

"Ya never know."

"Yep, ya never know. That's why they play the games. Ya don't win 'em on paper . . . or based on what the talking heads say."

*

The harsh December wind smacked DeAndre in the face as he walked toward his car. He tugged on the draw strings of his hoodie to close it tighter around his head. As he reached into his pocket for his car keys, a thought suddenly struck him.

Yeah . . . sure . . . that would work, and I'd have enough time afterwards to get away. And who'd know it was me because of the crowd surge. Because of the pandemonium that would occur . . . and with this one I could get away clean. And probably be a hero to boot! I mean if Kim Jung Un and the Russians can do it and get away with it, why not me?

Part One: Short Stories

Sunday, January 3, 10:30 p.m.

DeAndre Hawkins flew to Cleveland a day in advance of the president's downtown rally. Despite the forecast of a bone-chilling day, a crowd of up to 10,000 was expected. Following the rally, the president planned to meet with Ohio's governor to demand a recount based on an alleged ballot-box destruction in Dayton.

DeAndre checked in at the downtown Marriott. He'd booked one of the top floor rooms overlooking Public Square.

Two FedEx packages were waiting for him. Both had been sent December 31st by him to himself at the hotel. Both were marked "Fragile. Handle with Extreme Care."

*

Alone in his suite, DeAndre silenced his cell phone (which he was never supposed to do), shut off the TV, called the front desk and asked that he not be disturbed. He hung the plastic privacy card on the outside doorknob of his room. He didn't want anything or anybody to bother him.

Nothing and nobody did.

Then he sat down at the table in the kitchenette and opened the FedEx packages. Very slowly and very carefully.

After he attached the thin filament wires of the device he'd removed from the first FedEx package, he carefully placed the fully connected item in an empty milk carton he'd brought with him. Then he adjusted a tiny switch on a wristband which he would wear instead of his regular wristwatch the following day. It was a wristband that closely resembled a wristwatch.

That done, he exhaled. Then he put on his jacket, put the milk carton very slowly and very carefully in a paper bag and went out for a stroll.

*

The president had come to Cleveland to bully the Ohio governor into calling for a recount of the Ohio election in view of the extremely close election results. He argued that the election results would be different if alleged missing ballots from Dayton were to be counted. There was no actual proof that ballots in Dayton were missing, of course; but, so the theory ran, an allegation repeated often and vociferously enough, just might work. Who really needed actual evidence if you had a good theory and you repeated it over and over until it gained acceptance and credibility. Until it sunk in with the public and they regarded it as factual.

And a raucous rally in downtown Cleveland in support of the president plus the missing ballots theory just might get the governor's attention. It certainly would be a none too subtle message to the governor that he should accede to the president's demand. Especially in a year when the governor was up for reelection.

Prior rallies in other cities had demonstrated that there was considerable popular support for the president. Most of his party were predisposed to the notion that the election results were fraudulent and that the president in fact had won. Indeed, that he'd won by a landslide. And a recount—especially one based upon an allegation of missing Dayton ballots—would be conclusive. The president had consistently claimed election fraud on numerous prior occasions, all without the benefit substantiating of evidence as multiple courts and recounts had determined; but this time, he was convinced things would be different. Proving that Dayton ballots had been mishandled would reverse his string of defeats and set the record straight.

So he believed.

*

The rally was to be held in Public Square right across the street from the Marriott. The governor and other dignitaries would be there to welcome the president. The city's mayor and most of the city council members would not. They were all Democrats.

*

DeAndre nodded to the policeman and the junior Secret Service agent who stood at the corner of West Superior and West Roadway as he started his stroll around Public Square.

"If you don't mind, I'd like to check the perimeter," DeAndre said to the young agent. It was not necessary for DeAndre to show the young agent his ID. The young man had seen DeAndre's picture hanging in the foyer of the Secret Service dormitory in Washington. And he recalled seeing the video of DeAndre's saving Vice President Chadwick's life in 2003 in his training program.

"We've already done that, sir." The young agent replied. "Twice in fact."

"I knew you'd already have done that," DeAndre said, "but I always like to check things myself just to be sure. You know, you can't go wrong by being too cautious. And there are a lot of folks in this town that are pretty upset with the election results."

"Yes, Sir," the young agent replied. "Go ahead, Sir. I'll continue to keep watch."

DeAndre walked around the Public Square perimeter, stopping every now and then to scan the rope line, the rows of seats and the statue in the center of the square.

Halfway around the square, DeAndre stopped at a trash receptacle and glanced around. He saw the young agent looking the other way down West Superior. The policeman, too, was diverted. He was sipping coffee while leaning against his squad car.

After DeAndre had carefully and slowly lowered the milk carton into the otherwise empty trash receptacle, he completed his stroll around the perimeter of Public Square.

"Everything looks good," he said to the young agent as he returned to the Marriott.

"Yes, Sir. We've got it under control. Everything's all set, Sir."

"Cool. You've done a good job."

"Thank you, Sir. Have a good night, Sir."

"Thanks. You too. And good luck tomorrow. I hope the day will be uneventful."

Monday, January 4, 7:05 a.m.

DeAndre awoke as the sun started to slant in through his bedroom window. He never drew the curtains or shut the blinds when he was on the road or at home. *Who's gonna look in? And what if they do? What are they gonna see? Besides, I wanna see the sun come up. See the start of the new day. The fresh, new beginning. Maybe today's gonna be better than yesterday was. Then, too, I need to see what the weather's like. Assess what I might have to deal with.*

DeAndre thought about immediately getting up, but he continued to lie in the bed, staring at the ceiling. Thinking about this particular day. And what lay ahead. *This won't be like any ordinary day. This day's gonna be like November 23, 1963, or like September 11, 2001. This day's gonna be one that'll be remembered and it sure as hell is gonna be eventful.*

As he lay there thinking, meditating, going over the various steps he'd carefully planned, DeAndre was resolved. He knew what he had to do. For his country. For the Constitution he had sworn to uphold and safeguard. For what fate had determined that he alone should do. For what he, DeAndre Hawkins, he a simple, solitary Black man, the great-grandson of slaves, was chosen by destiny to do and do with firm commitment and resolve.

With that, DeAndre turned on his side, shot his feet out from under the covers and decisively rolled out of bed. He went to the window and looked down from the 27th floor. Crowds were already beginning to assemble along the rope lines. DeAndre could see the puffs of their breath rising in the chilly, early morning January air wafting in from Lake Erie. DeAndre noted the Cleveland policemen, the Ohio National

Guard and, of course, his own Secret Service detail assembled along the rope lines surrounding Public Square facing outward toward the gathering crowd.

Monday, January 4, 10:40 a.m.

DeAndre glanced at the bedside clock and saw that the time was 10:40 a.m. Time to go. He spoke into his headset and told his detail—the president's Secret Service team—to immediately assemble in the hotel lobby. The scheduled time for the proceedings to start was 11:00. For the president, however, DeAndre knew that 11:00 really meant 11:20. The converse of Lombardi time. Rather than the famous Green Bay Packers coach wanting his team to be ten minutes early, the president always wanted to keep everyone waiting. At least ten, and preferably twenty minutes. That, in his mind, would heighten the drama, heighten the sense of his importance. That was when the president would be ready to go.

Nevertheless, DeAndre knew his Secret Service contingent had to be in place at 10:50. They'd have to endure the president's pretentious, unnecessary delay just like everyone else.

After alerting his team, DeAndre picked up the wristband which resembled a wristwatch and wrapped it around his left wrist. Then he opened the second FedEx package he'd sent ahead to the hotel. This contained a small, glass vial of liquid securely wrapped in aluminum foil surrounded on all sides by Styrofoam and further securely covered with bubble wrap. Relieved that the vial hadn't broken, DeAndre carefully unwrapped it, put it in a special, rubberized pouch, surrounded the pouch with the bubble wrap and slipped the pouch into the left pocket of his jacket. He did so wearing thick rubber gloves.

*

"Well, let's go," the president barked as he got off the elevator and noticed DeAndre standing there awaiting his arrival. "What the fuck are you guys waiting for?"

It was 11:20. Precisely twenty minutes after the scheduled time for the president to make his triumphal, grand entry.

DeAndre nodded respectfully. "All set, Sir. We're already to go, Sir."

"Is everyone out there? The governor? Senator Bowen? The State majority leader?"

"Yes Sir. They're all there and in their seats awaiting your arrival, Sir."

"No Democrats from the City Council and not the mayor, I trust."

"No Sir. None of them. No Democrats."

"Good. I don't want any of them bastards to be there. How's the crowd? Good numbers? Did I get a good turn out?"

"Yes, Sir. They're anxiously awaiting your appearance, Sir. As for the number, I don't have an exact count for that, Sir. It's too early to get that. But the crowd looks quite sizeable. Eight, nine, perhaps ten or eleven rows deep all around the perimeter, Sir. And the chief of police estimates it will be at least seven to eight thousand. The media has the number somewhat higher. Fox estimates as many as ten thousand. They're probably a bit on the high side, however. Anyway, it's a good turnout for such a chilly day like today, Sir. Given that it's the first Monday in January."

"Good. Damn well better be given all that we've done for this town. You know, the RNC convention we held here in 2016, not to mention the special efforts we went to in removing the drop-boxes for mail-in ballots last fall," the president remarked quietly to himself, cupping his hand over his mouth so his comments couldn't be heard. To DeAndre, however, the president's words were clearly audible.

"Well, let's go then," the president commanded once again. "What the fuck are you waiting for?"

"Yes, Sir. Right this way, Sir." DeAndre replied, gesturing toward the front door and the red carpet, which had just been brushed to sweep away the light dusting of snow that had fallen in the last hour.

"I'll follow you, Sir."

The crowd erupted with cheers and loud applause as soon as the president emerged from the hotel into the open air.

Dropping his frown and scowl, the president smiled broadly and waved both arms high above his head. Then he took off his gloves and gave a thumbs-up sign with both hands. A slight breeze twirled the scarf around his neck.

DeAndre followed close behind the president and just to his right. He scanned the crowd, searching for any potential trouble as did his Secret Service colleagues ahead and behind the president.

As the president approached the steps to the platform where the governor and the other dignitaries were now standing and clapping, relieved that they didn't have to sit quietly in the cold awaiting the president's grand appearance any longer, DeAndre Hawkins pushed back the left sleeve of his jacket and pressed the switch on the little look-a-like wristwatch device strapped to his left wrist.

Immediately, there was a loud blast from the trash receptacle on the other side of Public Square.

Pandemonium broke out. Glass showered down from the buildings adjacent to Public Square. The crowd screamed and ran for cover helter-skelter. The dignitaries on the stage ducked for cover.

The moment the blast went off, DeAndre Hawkins tackled the president, covering him with his body. As he lay on top of the president, sheltering him from the cascading glass, he unzipped the pouch he was carrying in the left pocket of his jacket, uncapped the vial and poured its contents onto a handkerchief. Then he placed the handkerchief over the president's face. He did this quickly wearing thick rubber gloves.

"So you won't inhale any toxic dust, Mr. President. Are you okay, Mr. President?" DeAndre asked while quickly stuffing the handkerchief under the steps to the platform.

"Yes, yes, DeAndre! Thank you for protecting me! For saving my life! I heard all about you saving Chadwick's life and now you've done the same for me. Thank you! Thank you, DeAndre! Thank you!"

Monday, January 4, 5:56 p.m.

Later that day, the president, having complained of dizziness on the flight from Cleveland back to Washington, was taken to Walter Reed Hospital in Bethesda, Maryland for what was thought would be a routine checkup. It was there when his condition suddenly took a turn for the worse. And it was there when, despite extraordinary efforts to save his life, he died.

His wife, his second son, (not Junior, who was off in Dubai) and his Chief of Staff, Mack Sullivan, were at his bedside when the respirator to which he was hooked up went "beeeeeeeep."

Until a nurse came in and shut it off.

Two minutes later, a doctor came in, studied the president's unseeing eyes, then delicately closed the president's eyelids. "Boxcars," he said as he closed them. Later, he explained to the curious Mack Sullivan what the term "boxcars" referred to.

*

Two days later on January 6th, there was no storming of the Capital, and the House of Representatives routinely certified the results of the electoral college vote officially declaring that the challenger, Joseph Berens, had won. Two weeks after that, the inauguration was held on the steps of the Capitol Building where the new president was sworn in by the Chief Justice of the Supreme Court.

*

Part One: Short Stories

A week after the inauguration and following an intensive investigation, the Director of the FBI issued a report concluding that the president had died from the military-grade nerve agent, Novichok, which the Russians had invented and which they used on Aleksei Navalny the prior summer and on two former Russian spies in London three years prior to that. The report stated that although there had been a thorough investigation of all of the possible sources of the president's poisoning, the doorknobs he might have touched, the vehicles he may have ridden in, Air Force One and the various meeting rooms where post-election plans had been discussed, nothing conclusive was found to indicate the probable source of his poisoning.

The Marriott in Cleveland, of course, was thoroughly checked as was the forensic evidence gathered from Public Square. But nothing was found there either. The trash around the platform and the steps leading up to it had been thoroughly swept away immediately following the president's rally. So too, was DeAndre's wrinkled, dry, white handkerchief he'd stuffed under the stairs to the platform.

The FBI's statement speculated that the source of the poisoning was an undetermined foreign actor. Many in the media concluded that it was another example of Russian interference in American domestic affairs. Others in the media skeptically asked why the Russians would do such a thing after working so assiduously to get the president reelected in the first place. Putin vigorously denied any Russian involvement as did the Chinese and the North Koreans.

The consensus of the media was that it must have been someone at the hospital.

Fox News suggested it was someone associated with Antifa.

*

The afternoon following the rally, Tuesday, January 5th, DeAndre Hawkins got into his rented Chevy Malibu and headed east on I-90 toward Erie, Pennsylvania. Just over the Pennsylvania border, DeAndre stopped at a rest area and disposed of the empty glass vial and the rubber gloves he'd worn at Public Square in a trash receptacle.

In Erie, he dropped off the rental car and purchased a five-year-old Ford Taurus from a used car dealer who was more than happy to accept cash. At full sticker price with no haggling. After concluding that transaction, DeAndre turned onto I-79 and headed south to State Road 6, where he turned left and headed east.

State Road 6 spans the northern rim of Pennsylvania dotted by numerous small towns and hamlets. When he reached Galeton, DeAndre turned right on Route 144 and headed south until he came to the bridge across Kettle Creek—the "Project" the locals called it. There, he turned off Route 144 and went into seclusion.

He had arrived at "Socks's" cabin.

*

The sun sets early on January evenings in the Pennsylvania hill country, and it was pitch dark when DeAndre reached his destination.

"Sure hope Socks hasn't sold that cabin." DeAndre said to himself as he pulled into the hard-packed, dirt driveway. "And if he has, I hope he didn't tell the new owner about the key over the shutter to the right of the front door."

Part One: Short Stories

It was a quarter past nine and the only eyes that had seen DeAndre pulling off Route 144 were those of a white-tailed deer who bounded off the highway and into the protective forest when she saw the oncoming beams of the Ford's headlights. "So much for the 'deer frozen in the headlights' theory," DeAndre muttered as he turned in.

*

Socks's place was a hunting cabin in Potter County, Pennsylvania, sixteen miles south of Galeton. DeAndre's father had rented it from his Jersey buddy, Antonio "Socks" Brandisio, for several summers as a fishing getaway alongside Kettle Creek, a north-south tributary of the Susquehanna River.

DeAndre had gone there the last year the senior Hawkins went trout fishing at Kettle Creek. While very close friends of DeAndre's father might have associated him with Socks's cabin, no one would have made that connection with respect to DeAndre. Few, if any, even remembered that DeAndre had gone trout fishing with his father twenty-six years previously. But DeAndre remembered. And for him, Socks's cabin was the perfect hideout.

Perfect, too, in that it was only a few hundred miles from Cleveland.

*

Sure enough, the front door key to Socks's cabin was right where DeAndre remembered. So too was DeAndre's recollection that Socks kept a larder of canned baked beans, tomato soup, and spaghetti and meatballs in the kitchen cupboard. And, what he'd really hoped for, a jar of Maxwell House instant coffee and a case of Yuengling in the corner between the fridge and the kitchen sink.

Should be okay for food and coffee for a week or so anyway. By that time, the investigation should pretty much be over. The conspiracy theories will have run their courses, here as well as in Germany, Switzerland, South Africa, and wherever, DeAndre reasoned. *Everybody's got a 'McDonalds drive-thru attention span' these days and they'll be onto some other hot topic by next week, so I should be safe after that.*

And the Taurus? That's staying outta sight in Socks's garage. If I need something, I'll walk to Cross Forks. It's just down the road a bit. That should be pretty safe. Nobody pays much attention to TV news in Cross Forks anyway. Probably not even the news relating to the futile search for the president's killer. They'll be more interested in what the Pennsylvania Fish and Game Commission does with the regulations for the next bear hunting season.

And as for me, the letter I mailed to the Secret Service from Cleveland saying that I'm retiring and am going off to the northern Michigan woods, or perhaps to Montana or maybe even to Saskatchewan to live out my days, that should suffice for my severance from the Service. No one's really gonna care about me anyway. The country will be on to other 'BREAKING NEWS' and the former president's death will slowly fade from the headlines.

So, I'm gonna get away clean. Clean and forgotten and with my reputation intact.

Part One: Short Stories

June 9, Cross Forks, Pennsylvania

DeAndre wasn't particularly concerned about being identified in Cross Forks, Potter County, Pennsylvania.

The main event in Cross Forks during the summer was the annual rattlesnake hunt held on the 4th of July. That's when many people came to Cross Forks from the surrounding towns and counties. But that event wouldn't be for several weeks yet so he wasn't worried that he'd be recognized by any ardent rattlesnake hunter.

Similarly, there was little chance that any of the locals would identify him because their TV watching was pretty much limited to game shows and soap operas. Furthermore, he had no worries about his picture being posted on the town's mini-post office bulletin board. There wouldn't be room for that on account of the pin-up ads for the sale of used cars, the local church's bake sale and, of course, announcements for the annual rattlesnake hunt.

Priorities had to be observed and respected. Traditions had to be maintained. So DeAndre felt he was safe from discovery.

*

It was a warm early summer day in June and DeAndre's cancer had progressed to the point where he ached with pain all over his body and rarely got up from his bed. But thinking that the warmth of the sun and some fresh air might do him some good, he struggled out of bed and staggered out into the woods next to Socks's cabin.

He'd heard a woodpecker drumming away on a dead tree out there and he wondered if it was the colorful giant downy red that he'd seen days before.

Not finding the bird and feeling weary, DeAndre lay down on a bed of soft pine needles waiting for the woodpecker to commence his drumming once again.

As he lay there, he listened to the soft rustling of a breeze whispering through the tops of the pines. It was a beautiful, peaceful sound. A sound that he loved. A sound like hushed tones of violins. A sound that was restful and put him at ease.

He spread his arms out wide like he'd done as a child in wintertime making angel wings in fresh fallen snow.

*

Angelic, that was the way the two sophomores from Penn State found him on the 4th of July weekend.

They found no rattlesnakes that day—only the body of the unsuspected assassin of America's Demagogue-in-Chief. The assassin, who in the public's eye and more importantly in the eyes of his colleagues at the Secret Service, remained one of the Service's all-time heroes. A hero for having saved the life of a vice-president in 2003; and then, years later, for temporarily saving the life of the president himself. He was the only man in the history of the Secret Service to have accomplished such feats.

Part One: Short Stories

It simply was unfortunate that, inexplicably, somehow an illegal immigrant from Guatemala, who worked as a maintenance man at Walter Reed, had managed to poison the president despite DeAndre Hawkins's heroic endeavors earlier that day.

MY UNCLE SAL

written with the assistance of Elizabeth A. Horn

Looking back from where I stand today, I can see things more clearly. But back then—when I was just a kid—my perception of reality and of my Uncle Sal was sprinkled with pigtails, Eskimo Pies, and root beer floats at Pitt's Goodie Shoppe. Little did I really know about my uncle, who he really was and what he really did. No one in the family ever talked about stuff like that.

To me, he was just my adorable uncle.

And to him, I was just his adorable niece. I knew I was his favorite. It was obvious and indisputable because of what he did for me. And for what he didn't do for others—for my sisters, my brother, and my cousins. Besides, that's what everyone in my family said.

Let me begin when I was ten. That was the year my uncle died.

*

For starters, it's important for you to know a little bit about my family and me. My father was Irish, and he worked as a lineman for the phone company. My mother was Italian. She was the youngest of Uncle Sal's five sisters. She herself had five kids: a boy, the oldest, and four

Part One: Short Stories

daughters. I, being the youngest, was the "baby of the family." It was a role I loved and—to tell the truth—one that I exploited.

We lived on West Erie Avenue, the same street as Uncle Sal and his wife, Aunt Rose. Our house was two blocks from theirs in the lower part of the town.

Oh, I forgot to tell you the name of the town, Elmira, New York. Technically, Elmira is a city, but that was just a formal designation. In reality, it was a "town" and had the feel of a small, intimate little community. It's in the southern part of New York state. The "Southern Tier," they call it. It's just a few miles from the Pennsylvania border.

*

My mom and Uncle Sal had lots of relatives in Pennsylvania, mainly in the eastern part, in Wilkes-Barre, Scranton and a few in Philadelphia. Uncle Sal used to make frequent trips to Philly, "On business" he'd say. He never said what kind of business. And back then I didn't much care. It wasn't until I was in college at Cornell that I found out. A sorority sister of mine from Philly, a girl of Italian descent like me, clued me in.

Anyway, back to my story, I clearly was the favorite niece of Uncle Sal, and for that matter, of his wife, Aunt Rose. While Uncle Sal had lots of nieces to choose from, I knew early on that I was special in his eyes. This always endeared me toward Uncle Sal. Still does. Even today. Despite what I now know.

How did I know I was his favorite? He never said so specifically, but it was pretty obvious from the special things he did for me. Things where he singled me out from the others. Things like taking me—just me—to get ice cream in the summertime to Pitt's Goodie Shoppe on Pennsylvania Avenue just a few blocks from our house. It was real close to Southside High. It was where if someone said, "You're in the Pitt's," they weren't putting you down. It was an extracurricular, razzamatazz, happening type of a place. And even though it was primarily a hangout for kids, Uncle Sal would take me there because he knew I liked it and—perhaps more importantly—because it was close to his club and one of his business interests, Agbe Novelties, which was right across the street from Pitt's. More about his club and Agbe Novelties later.

Anyway, Pitt's was where Uncle Sal liked to take me. But before he did, he'd call my home, speak to my mom, tell her he felt like going out for a walk and would it be okay if he took me along. He was always respectful of my parents' authority, particularly that of my mother. The chain of command of the family had to be respected. That was his code. And in my family, my mother was the first link in that chain. Uncle Sal tolerated my father; but, since he was Irish, not Italian, it was only a form of sufferance which was a long way from respect or brotherhood—even brother-in-law-hood.

But Uncle Sal's fondness for me was more than just summertime afternoon strolls for ice cream. Much more. Many nights I'd sleep over at his and Aunt Rose's even though I lived just down the street. And I was the only one who had that privilege. None of my sisters or cousins ever had that honor. And certainly not my brother who became a priest. Even as a child, he was somewhat effeminate, manifesting traits that we'd later call "gay." Traits my Uncle Sal abhorred.

It was always fun at Uncle Sal's and Aunt Rose's.

Their house sat quite a bit back from the street with a big front yard and an even bigger back yard. It sat on a rise—a small hill—that elevated it above the other houses on the street. Now that I think about it, it had kind of a commanding position over the other houses. I suppose that's one reason why Uncle Sal wanted to live there.

There was an arrow-tipped, white picket fence beside the sidewalk and around the sides of the yard. I remember that Uncle Sal said the pointed tips on the wooden slats were to keep the birds from sitting there. Although robins never did, sometimes smaller birds, like sparrows, alighted there. I liked it when they did.

In the middle of the front yard was a small statue of the Virgin Mary, her arms spread wide, welcoming and receiving, a beloved religious figure. Aunt Rose insisted that she be there.

The back yard was much larger than the front. Uncle Sal and Aunt Rose had quite a vegetable garden there. Uncle Sal liked to "putter around" in the garden on his days off in the summertime, but it was Aunt Rose who mostly tended it. They grew tomatoes, green beans, onions, cucumbers and even some herbs. You know, stuff that would make good sauce for pasta. "Gravy," Uncle Sal called it. I never thought of Aunt Rose's pasta sauce as "gravy." To me it was simply sauce. But Uncle Sal always called it "gravy", and no one ever corrected him. Not my mother, not Aunt Rose and certainly not my father. So "gravy" it was. And I didn't care what Uncle Sal called it. I just knew it tasted good. That was all that really mattered.

At the far rear of the property, at the crest of the hill, there was a wooden shed. I especially remember that. It wasn't kept up very well.

Paint was peeling and the door was on the back side facing the rear of the property. You couldn't see the door from the house or the garden or even from the street on the other side because of a tall hedge. I was always curious about the shed. But my oldest sister told me never to ask about it and certainly to never go there. So, I never did. Later I learned what Uncle Sal kept inside. Yes, there were some gardening tools, but mostly there were other things that he used in his business. The shed was always locked, and Uncle Sal had the only key.

To the left of the shed, Uncle Sal and Aunt Rose had a chicken coop. And one for rabbits too. That is, until they were ready for a stew. On those days—when the rabbits were "selected"—I wasn't allowed to visit. I loved those little bunnies and missed them when I was told that one or two "had escaped." I never thought about how they escaped or where they escaped to; I never thought about where the little chunks of meat in Aunt Rose's stew came from.

The interior of the house was typical of the neighborhood homes in that era: large living and dining rooms, and a kitchen with a staircase leading up to the bedrooms. As was typical of Catholic homes, there was a cross on the staircase wall and a portrait of Jesus with the bleeding heart. An enclosed front porch spanned the entire front of the house. It had a pullout sofa that converted into a bed. That's where I slept when I stayed over.

Further down the street, on the other side of the rise was St. Monica's Catholic Church. It was a red brick, traditional kind of church, unlike the majestic soaring cathedral in the main part of town. It did have a lovely sounding bell though. I specifically remember that. The bell started ringing very early Sunday mornings at six and every hour on the hour thereafter until noon. It was such a beautiful, tolling sound soaring above the rooftops and the trees. I loved that sound even though it woke me up much earlier than I wanted.

*

As I said, Uncle Sal was the undisputed head of the family. But when it came to running the house, well, that was a different story. In that case, he always deferred to Aunt Rose. With respect to household matters and decisions, she had exclusive jurisdiction. The house was her domain.

Aunt Rose was the typical, "mature" Italian matriarch. She was ample of figure with heavy, robust arms. And she almost always wore an apron; and, as I recall, she never was without a narrow black ribbon on top of her head to keep her hair in place. On Sundays, she always wore a mantilla to church.

Aunt Rose had a ready smile, a quick wit and a deep alto, commanding voice. She wasn't much for idle chatter; but when she talked, we all listened. Even Uncle Sal. Although he did wink at us occasionally when Aunt Rose veered into what he called "women's talk" relating to the goings on at St. Monica's or in the neighborhood. Although he silently tolerated it, Uncle Sal wasn't much for gossip or petty neighborhood issues. He dealt with "big picture" matters and concerns relating to his business.

Mostly, Aunt Rose spoke in English; but sometimes, when she didn't want us children to understand, she'd revert to the language of the "old country" as she called it. She'd do that especially with Uncle Sal if she had difficulty finding the right English words to express her thoughts. And she'd do so on other occasions as well. If someone said or did something she didn't approve of or that she thought was just plain wrong, she'd look directly at the miscreant and render her judgment succinctly in Italian: "Stupida!" Even sometimes when it was Uncle Sal who she thought had erred. She was the only one who had the audacity to make such a pronouncement pertaining to him.

*

Aunt Rose was the oldest of five sisters. Her parents, Nicolo and Philomena, had immigrated from Mondello, Sicily, just north of Palermo, in the late 1890s. Their grainy photographs were on the wall above the handrail on the staircase. There were no photographs of Uncle Sal's parents, or of any of his brothers or sisters. I don't know when they immigrated to the United States or exactly where they came from. It was general knowledge, however, that they'd come from some place in Sicily, most likely Palermo. Lots of Italians immigrated from southern Italy and Sicily in the days before World War I.

But, back to Aunt Rose: my favorite recollections of her were the times I'd curl up on her lap and she'd read to me on sleep-over nights. Usually, they were Nancy Drew stories. Sometimes Anne of Green Gables. Those were my favorites. While reading these stories, Aunt Rose would frequently interrupt with anecdotes about her childhood. Sometimes they were relevant to the story's narrative, but most often they were not. The ones that were not were always more intimate and informative. Those were the ones I liked best. Those were the ones that told me about her. I really, really loved my Aunt Rose.

*

Sundays were always special at Uncle Sal's and Aunt Rose's. The whole family would gather around noon; mom and dad, my four siblings and me, two of my mother's sisters, their husbands and seven cousins. All told, twenty of us. Eight adults and the four oldest grandchildren ate in the dining room and the eight younger grandchildren, me included, were seated at card tables in the living room.

It was a lively, boisterous group with lots of laughter, storytelling and, yes, gesticulation. Sometimes, it seemed like everyone was talking at once. Except for Uncle Sal. He always sat quietly at the head of the table at the far end of the dining room. Aunt Rose was always seated to his left. Normally, he had a slight, contented smile on his face. You could just tell he basked in the warmth of his family; he, the patriarch, the master of his clan. The only time he frowned was when one of my other uncles—his brothers-in-law, and particularly my father—had the temerity to voice their opinions. Fortunately, those occasions were rare and usually quite brief.

To my uncles and my father at those Sunday dinners, my Uncle Sal was a force of nature. My father and uncles would stop what they were talking about and shut up right in mid-sentence if he gave just a look or a grunt. He exuded that much power and command by a mere glance. Even his mere presence had an arresting effect. It was an aura that he had. How a man of such strength and power had so much sensitivity and was capable of so much love amazed me at the time. It still does. Even to this very day. Especially on account of what I now know.

*

Dinner usually consisted of heaping, steaming bowls of spaghetti with meatballs, Italian hot sausage, chicken parts and often pork loin for flavor. Sometimes there were other ingredients too. Probably rabbit meat now that I think about it. Aunt Rose's sauce, the "gravy," was made from the tomatoes and herbs she grew in her garden. She canned it and kept the jars in the cellar until it was needed for the pasta.

And, of course, there was wine; quantities of wine. Chianti and Montepulciano.

On nice days in the summertime, we dined outside on long tables set up in the backyard in front of the garden.

*

I especially liked my days with Aunt Rose and Uncle Sal—particularly those days in summer when school was out, and I had more time to spend with them. More nights when I got to sleep over.

In the late summer, when the vegetables were ripe, Aunt Rose and I would pick them. As I mentioned, there were tomatoes, onions, cucumbers, and green beans too. I particularly remember the green beans. I'd tug them off the plant, then snip off the stems. In addition, there were herbs that Aunt Rose needed to make her sauce. I loved to help her make it in the big iron pot she almost always had simmering on the stove. "The sauce is not to be rushed," she used to say, "it needs to marinate and season."

*

Aunt Rose always treated me like the daughter she never had. Most Saturdays in the summer, she'd deviate from her normal, daily routine and take me to the afternoon matinee at Elmira's RKO Theater. Back then, it was usually a double feature. In those days, there was no such thing as Red Box movie dispensers. No Netflix or Hulu either. You went to an actual theater to see a movie instead.

Sometimes, however, we'd go shopping instead of the movies. Aunt Rose loved to buy me clothes. "I need to dress you up," she'd say. "Your mother, my sister-in-law, has no taste for clothes or perhaps she doesn't have the money . . . Dear, don't you tell her I said that!" She'd always admonish.

Anyway, these were some of the reasons I liked spending time with Aunt Rose.

*

Now let me turn to the wonderful things Uncle Sal did for me. Like Aunt Rose, he thought of me as his daughter. "My little girl" he used to call me. "Come here, my little one," he'd say. And when I went to him, he'd give me the biggest hug ever. Then he'd put his arm around my shoulders and continue to hold me close. I loved it when he did that. It made me feel warm and loved. It made me feel special. It was something my own father never did. I suppose he was too busy or too tired from work. Or maybe it was because he had so many other children and he didn't want to single out any one of us. Perhaps he didn't want to show any favoritism. I don't really know. I just know that it didn't happen the way it happened with my Uncle Sal.

And now that I think about it, there was one other special thing Uncle Sal did for me. Something singular that really, really stood out and wasn't just routine or ordinary like going to Pitt's Goodie Shoppe for ice cream. In April of '57 I think it was, the Chemung—that's the river that flows through Elmira—overflowed and flooded the city and the surrounding countryside. Water was everywhere. The streets were no longer really streets; they were canals. People used canoes and small boats to get from one place to another instead of cars. Stores and banks and businesses were closed, boarded up. But it didn't do any good. The water still got in. Even Keuka Lake, a big, deep lake just a few miles north of Elmira — one of New York State's "Finger Lakes" —flooded. People who owned lakefront cottages had lake trout swimming in their living rooms.

And our home, like others, wasn't spared. But Uncle Sal's and Aunt Rose's did escape because it was higher up. Ours, however, along with our immediate neighbors and even St. Monica's, got flooded. Particularly our basement. It was a big, indoor bathtub filled to the brim.

That's where our playroom was. And that's where I had my dollhouse and my family of dolls. That's where the flood really impacted me. All my dolls and dollhouse furniture were floating on the surface of our indoor lake and my dollhouse itself was completely submerged. And the worst thing for me anyway—mind you I was only six at the time—was that my favorite doll, a Raggedy Ann cloth doll with the button eyes, got swept away in the flood. Or perhaps it just sank and got thrown out when the clean-up crew came in after the waters subsided.

Anyway, Raggedy Ann was missing, and I never found her. I was crushed. Heartbroken. It was like my best friend had drowned and I'd never see her again.

Knowing that I was grieving over the loss of Raggedy Ann, Uncle Sal took me to all of the stores in Elmira where dolls and dollhouses were sold the Saturday following the flood in order to find a replacement. We went everywhere. But we couldn't find one. Only one store had a Raggedy Ann, and it was too small. Besides, it was made of plastic. My Raggedy was bigger and made of cloth. So, the plastic one—the only Raggedy in Elmira—just wouldn't do. It was totally unacceptable, and I cried and cried and stomped my foot and I insisted I didn't want it. In truth, looking back now, I was probably just being a spoiled little brat; but anyway, Uncle Sal didn't get upset with me. He understood and he put his big arm around me and held me close and said, "not to worry, 'cuz we're gonna go to another city . . . a bigger city that has bigger stores . . . and we'll be sure to find you the right kind of Raggedy Ann there." He was wonderful: truly, truly wonderful.

And that's what we did. The very next Saturday he took me all the way to Philadelphia where I'd never been before, and we found a true Raggedy Ann at Wanamaker's just like my drowned Raggedy. She was exactly the same, an identical twin. A twin with the same button eyes, the same curly red hair and she was made from the same cloth just like my Raggedy. I was thrilled, ecstatic when I found her. I remember jumping up and down for joy and running down the aisles of Wanamakers. I almost ran into an old lady shopping with her granddaughter. The granddaughter—who was probably eight—frowned at me. But Uncle Sal didn't seem to mind. He didn't get upset. He just smiled and whispered something to the old lady. I also remember him handing her something . . . something small, like a note of apology. Now that I think about it, it undoubtedly was money. Anyway, the old lady seemed happy, and she quickly took her granddaughter to another part of the store.

Uncle Sal said it was no problem for him to take me to Philadelphia because he had business there.

When he was out attending to business that evening, I stayed with one of my other aunts, Uncle Sal's sister, Lucinda, and my cousins. I remember that was a fun time too, especially with my new Raggedy Ann. She slept with me the whole night long.

Needless to say, that Raggedy Ann experience endeared me even more to Uncle Sal. To me, he was just a big, old softy. A cream puff. And I was his little girl. He loved me and he hugged me. He made me feel really, really special. Really, really loved. And I know my love for him made him feel special too.

Such a wonderful, tender, gentle, sensitive, loving man, he was. My Uncle Sal.

*

Part One: Short Stories

As I mentioned, Uncle Sal had businesses in Wilkes-Barre, Scranton, and Philadelphia in Pennsylvania as well as in Binghamton, Corning and Elmira, New York. The meetings in Philly were more significant because those always involved overnight stays whereas the ones in Wilkes-Barre and Scranton did not. I didn't really know why. Remember, I was just a kid at the time. A kid absorbed with kid things. And when you're a kid, you don't really care why or where an uncle of yours stays or what he does while he's away on business.

And as I mentioned, my family didn't talk about Uncle Sal's business. Perhaps they, like me, were concerned with only the things that pertained to their lives and didn't much care about what Uncle Sal did because it didn't concern them. Or perhaps not, perhaps they simply preferred not to talk about what he did. I don't really know. And it doesn't much matter now.

*

Anyway, this much I do know. Uncle Sal had a small business in Elmira. As I mentioned earlier, he owned a store called Agbe Novelties just across the street from Pitts' Goodie Shoppe on Pennsylvania Avenue. While it featured greeting cards, it also had stuffed animals, teddy bears, toy airplanes, toy cars and trucks, and electric trains. Novelties and stuff like that.

But my favorite item in Agbe's was a kid-size, little pink rocking horse. When I was really little, I used to ride it every time I was there and I used to beg Uncle Sal to take me there so I could ride it. Later on, when I got to be bigger at about age eight or nine, it was beneath me to ride it. Then it was just for little kids.

Looking back at it now, it strikes me as curious why I never questioned why it wasn't sold. After all, if I liked it so much, wouldn't other little kids also have liked it? Wouldn't they have begged their parents to buy it? At the time though, I never asked why. Now, I think I know why. It probably was because no other little kids ever saw it or ever rode on it. Because no other little kids ever went into Agbe Novelties. I was the only kid who did. And that was only on account of my Uncle Sal being the owner.

Although no kids ever went into Agbe's, lots of other people did. Mostly men. Sometimes even policemen. In fact, quite a few policemen did and that always struck me as somewhat odd. Why so many cops? There never were any incidents there that I ever heard of. No holdups, no break-ins and no disturbances of any sort. In any event, I never thought to ask why so many cops went there. I guess I just took comfort knowing that my uncle's business was well protected by the police.

While mostly it was men, now and then a woman would go in. Usually, an older one with a fancy lace hat curious to see what was for sale, or perhaps to buy something for a grandchild. But they were never in there very long and I never saw any of them come out with purchases. Furthermore, I never saw any of them go in a second time.

Sometimes, however, younger women went in. I remember seeing girls who'd just graduated from high school or who went to a nearby college go in. Once I recognized two girls who'd been in my oldest sister's graduating class at high school. They were dressed differently this time, kind of flashy, if you know what I mean. Not like they dressed for high school; you know, not wearing bobby socks and plaid, full skirts, which were popular back in those days.

But those girls never went in through the front door. They always parked their cars, or were dropped off in the parking lot next to Agbe's and went around the rear of the shop to enter through the back door. They must have stayed there quite a while because I never saw any of them leave. Of course, I didn't sit around at Pitts waiting for them to leave. I didn't want my ice cream to melt and I wasn't that curious anyway.

There were, as I mentioned, lots of men who frequented Agbe's. Ordinary men. Usually, they were alone. I'd see them going in when I was sitting in Pitt's across the street after school and in the summertime when the weather was nice. I always sat by the window in Pitt's, so I could see what was going on out on the street. That's how I saw who went in and out of Agbe's.

It wasn't until years later that I figured out why the men never came out with packages.

*

Uncle Sal also went to what he called his "club". It really wasn't a club. It was just a restaurant that had a bar. It was called "The Quill" and it was on State Street. Uncle Sal never took me there and neither did my parents. Once, when I asked if we could go there for dinner sometime, my mother said, "No, Dear, that's where your uncle does his business and we don't want to bother him while he's working."

So that put an end to that.

I was really curious though, because as I've said, I really loved my Uncle Sal and I wanted to see where he worked. He went there quite often, usually late in the day and stayed well after dinnertime, so I figured he must have enjoyed dining there. Based on that, I assumed the food must be pretty good at The Quill. That's what I told my mom when she asked why I wanted to go there.

But that really wasn't the reason. The real reason was I just wanted to see the place where my favorite uncle went so often to conduct his business—whatever his business was.

So anyway, that's my story as a young girl. Now let me move ahead a few years, eight or nine years, to be a bit more precise.

*

I'm now a freshman at Cornell and I'm living in Balch Hall. I'm an art history major. I chose art history because of my Italian heritage and because I was enamored of the great Italian artists of the Renaissance era; Michelangelo, da Vinci, Caravaggio, and many of the others of that glorious era.

Well, it was about three weeks into our freshman year and my roommate, Carmella Salvaggio, and I are lying in our beds in our dorm room. It's, I don't know, probably sometime around 1:15 - 1:30 a.m. It could have been as late as 2:00 a.m. I don't know. And it really doesn't matter. Anyway, we were having this wonderful conversation. You know, one of those deep conversations where you're talking about anything and everything—all sorts of topics. No subjects barred. And it's best if they're intimate and personal. But they must be 100% honest—absolutely, 100% honest.

I don't remember now exactly which one of us started talking about our families, but one of us did. We were still getting to know one another at that point, and we hadn't really gotten into our respective families to any great extent—just superficial stuff up—none of the really good family dirt. You know, like the black sheep in your family, some of the troubles your siblings got into, what some of your cousins were like, who you liked and didn't like. Stuff like that.

Anyway, Carmella was telling me about her brother and sister—both older than she—and how she was the first in her family to go to college. About how her brother Augie, who was a good athlete, but got kicked off the football team because he got one of the cheerleaders "in trouble," as she put it. When I asked her what sort of "trouble," she just tilted her head, looked at me quizzically and told me I was "pretty naive." As I think about it now, I guess I was pretty naive back then.

Then she told me about her father, how he started out as a mason, but eventually opened his own little company, which grew and grew and became a major construction firm in Philadelphia. How it built bridges and buildings and even did some runway renovations for the Philadelphia and Camden, New Jersey, airports. How he had problems with unions from time to time, but how he knew how to deal with "pretty rough characters," as she put it.

Then I told her about my family and that they were very normal and very boring. That we didn't have the glamour and pizazz that hers did. I told her about our petty sibling rivalries and how I was the baby of the family, a high school cheerleader, and how my sisters were always kind of jealous of me.

Eventually, I went on to tell her about my favorite relatives, Aunt Rose, and Uncle Sal. I explained that I was like the daughter they never had but really wanted. I told her how I'd often spend time at their house, about the sleepovers, the big Sunday dinners, about helping Aunt Rose make the pasta sauce, and about the Saturday afternoons when she'd take me to the movies and shopping.

Then, of course, I told her about how I loved my Uncle Sal and all the special things he did for me. That he was loving, gentle and sweet and that he'd take me to Pitt's Goodie Shoppe for ice cream and root beer floats, and how I'd watch the Agbe Novelties store. I also told her about the men and the cops who'd go in there and about the young women who'd always go in the back door.

At that point, Carmella got pretty interested as I recall. She rolled over, propped herself up on one elbow, put her hand over her lips and started to chuckle.

When she did that, I stopped telling her my story and asked what the matter was. Then she burst out laughing, waved her arms and told me to go on. So, I did.

I told her about the flood of '57 and about my Raggedy Ann doll that got washed away. And how my Uncle Sal was so kind, sensitive, gentle and understanding, and about how he took me to Iszard's Department Store in Elmira the first Saturday after the flood, but that we couldn't find the right Raggedy—just a cheap inferior one that was made out of plastic, not cloth, and that had painted-on features, not sewn on, real button eye—and how disappointed I was. And I told her how I cried and sobbed and said I didn't want that "stupid, fake Raggedy Ann" and how I wanted a "real one" like the one that I'd had.

Then I told her how my uncle was so kind and understanding, and how he comforted me and didn't get angry or frustrated like most people would—particularly men like my father. And I went on about him taking me to Wanamaker's in Philadelphia to get a real Raggedy because he was going there anyway to meet with some of his associates to plan for a big meeting coming up in a town in the Catskills called Appalachia in a couple of weeks. He said they needed to "establish their agenda" as he put it.

At that point, Carmella got even more excited, and she leapt out of bed, came over to mine and grabbed me by the shoulders and asked, "Your Uncle Sal . . . was his last name Magadino?" I was stunned; and, of course, I asked, "Yes, but how in the world did you know that? I never told you his last name. Just that his name was Sal, presumably for 'Salvatore'."

And so, then she starts shaking me and says "Whoa, whoa there, Gabby, whoa there. Do you have any idea who that sweet, sensitive, gentle, understanding uncle of yours really was?"

And I told her, "Sure, I knew him very well." That I knew what a good man he was. How tender and loving and affectionate he was and how he loved me and did all those special things for me and that I was like the daughter that he never had.

And then Carmella butted in again and stopped me from prattling on and on. She was calmer then and no longer shaking me and she asked, "Do you have any idea what kind of 'business' your Uncle Sal was in and what the so-called Agbe Novelty Shop really was. Then she told me that it was undoubtedly a bookie joint with guys coming in to place bets and then going upstairs to where the young women were for "a little matinee or an afternoon delight" before going home to their proper Episcopalian and Presbyterian wives and families in the suburbs, "after getting their rocks off." And how the cops went in to get their hush money "takes" and that was why no one ever left Agbe's with packages under their arms.

Then she asked—and this was the knockout question: "And do you know what your darling, sweet, loving, gentle uncle was really doing in Philadelphia and what the meeting in Appalachia, the meeting with Gambino, Costello and the others, was all about?"

I said, "No," of course; so she then went onto tell me what she knew about Salvatore Magadino, my Uncle Sal, and about Francesco Scarpellino, a/k/a "Frankie Scarp," who got whacked when he stepped outside of the Blue Gardenia Restaurant in Corning, New York early one morning. How the hit men then stuffed him in the trunk of his car and drove it to a backroad outside of Painted Post, New York, where they abandoned the car. How the State Troopers eventually caught one of the hitmen, Billy Sullivan, who the Mafia had recruited from Brooklyn to do the job, and how he testified that it was Salvatore Magadino who'd ordered the hit.

Then she went on to tell me how a Sammy G—she couldn't recall his last name, but that everyone called him "Sammy G"—left a steak house in Binghamton one night after dinner, got into his Lincoln, turned on the ignition and got blown to bits when a car bomb exploded. How the city cops and the state troopers investigated it but never could prove who was responsible. But how all the newspapers speculated that Salvatore Magadino probably had something to do with it because Sammy G. had just opened up his own bookie joint in downtown Binghamton that was encroaching on Salvatore Magadino's territory.

I, of course, was stunned. Incredulous. I simply couldn't believe it. This wasn't the kind, gentle, understanding and sensitive Uncle Sal that I knew and loved. And after recovering from my shock, I asked her how she knew all this and she said it was all over the news in Philadelphia at the time of the Appalachia bust and how she wrote a paper about it for her social studies class her senior year in high school. After she told me all of this, I rolled over in my bed, wide-eyed and silent for a long time. Finally, I started to cry, and Carmella laid down next to me and said, "Sorry, Gabby, I thought you probably knew all this."

*

After a while, I got up, dressed, and started toward the door.

Carmella said, "Wait Gabby, where are you going at this hour of the night?"

I told her I'd never be able to go to sleep that night and that I was going out for a walk, which I did.

I walked all around the campus. Down past the law school. Through College Town, then down Stewart to Cascadilla Street in the main part of town and that's where the campus police found me and brought me back to my dorm.

Carmella must have called them after I left. I never asked her afterwards. But she had to be the one who phoned 9-1-1.

She was probably worried that I might "gorge out." That's what the college kids called it when students jumped into one of the gorges bordering Cornell's campus. Students who couldn't take the pressure of college and decided to commit suicide.

*

So that's it. That's my story about my Uncle Sal.

THE RUSSIAN DESERTER

2:16 a.m., March 15, 2022
Honchariuske, a small town north of Kyiv in Ukraine

It was a light touch on her shoulder, but Kateryna felt it anyway. And it woke her. She rolled over and saw her nephew, Dmytro, five, standing at her bedside. A tear was meandering down his left cheek.

"What is it, Dear?" she asked.

"My tummy hurts," he replied.

"Did you go to your mommy?"

"Yes, but she told me to go back to sleep. I told her I couldn't and she said, 'then go see Aunt Kateryna because I need my sleep.'"

"Oh, okay." Kateryna replied as she rolled over and got out of bed.

*

Kateryna warmed some milk for Dmytro; and when he said his tummy didn't hurt quite so much, she gave him some cold milk and a slice of Medovik (classic Ukrainian honey cake).

When his eyes got heavy, she carried him back to bed.

Then she went back to the kitchen to put away the milk and blow out the lantern when she stopped cold in her tracks. A bolt of fear seized her. A shadow quickly darted out of sight outside the kitchen window—a man's shadow.

She went immediately to the back door, the door to the backyard and the barn. She knew she'd locked it before going to bed, but she wanted to check to be sure.

Sure enough, it was locked.

Still, she didn't feel safe.

She tiptoed silently into her father's room and went to the corner where he kept his Tokarev TT-33, his WWII pistol. Her father stirred but didn't wake up.

Kateryna went back to the kitchen and sat for several minutes. She didn't light the lantern. But she held the Tokarev firmly in her grasp.

She sat there in the dark for over twenty minutes. Nothing happened.

*

Did I just imagine it? Was I half asleep? Having a dream? Maybe that's it. Maybe I didn't really see it. Maybe I just dreamt it.

No, no. It wasn't a dream. You saw it. You know you did.

Kateryna waited still longer. She heard nothing. No squawking from the hen house. No mooing from the cows in the barn. No barking of the family's dog. So, she went back to bed.

But she took her father's pistol with her.

*

She'd been in bed, unable to sleep, for a half hour when she heard another sound. This time it wasn't little Dmytro, or his little sister, Nataliya, her niece; it was a tap, tap, tapping at her window.

Though it was dark in her room and outside, there was still enough moonlight that she could see a face pressed close to the glass.

She grabbed for the pistol, but something told her not to raise it. It was a scraggy, dirty, bearded face. A man's face. And his eyes were wide and desperate looking, but they did not look threatening. Though he had on a soldier's cap, Kateryna could tell that his hair was long and light in color.

He looked to be in his twenties, about the same age as she herself.

Kateryna simply stared at him. After several seconds, she moved her lips and hoped the soldier could read them through the glass.

"What do you want?" her lips said. They said it in Russian. In Kateryna's second language. The language she thought he might understand as she had heard there were break-away Russian soldiers in the neighborhood.

He jerked his head toward the back door.

Can I trust him? What if he rapes me? Kills my family? No, that's not what I saw in his eyes. Maybe I should see what he wants.

She nodded to the face, put on her robe, went to the kitchen. She approached the back door, reached for the bolt with her left hand and in her right, tightly grasped her father's pistol.

*

Believing that there were Russian soldiers roaming the woods in her neighborhood, deserters from a Russian tank convoy stalled on route M20 running between Chernihiv and Kyiv, Kateryna thought he might be one of them. She'd heard that the convoy had been halted, its tanks and support vehicles destroyed by Javelin and Sidewinder missiles supplied to the Ukrainian forces by the United States and its NATO allies. The convoy was running out of fuel, rations, and medicines. And more than being without material, they were running out of motivation. Most of them were young conscripts—some mere boys— many from the rural steppes of Russia who were disillusioned by the killing of innocent civilians and the destruction of cities and towns, residences and farms, schools and hospitals, even churches, which they were ordered to demolish—atrocities which they knew their mothers would deplore and never forgive.

Perhaps more importantly, they knew, too, that they'd been lied to. They recalled that their lieutenants and sergeants, their more immediate commanders, had told them they were merely going to be on a training mission and that it would only last for two or three days. And they'd heard that their generals and colonels, their very highest commanders, had said this was merely a "special operation." And they knew these statements weren't true. That they'd been lied to. Deliberately and intentionally lied to. That this wasn't just a "training mission" or a "special operation." It was a war. And furthermore, an immoral war, and a war that they were losing.

Some had only their uniforms, boots and minimal weapons and ammunition when they fled. All were rag-tag and desperate. They were desperate for food, bandages, medicines, and a warm place out of the cold where they could safely lie down and sleep. And, more than anything else, they were afraid—desperately afraid of the merciless and ruthless, GRU-trained, military police, who with their indefatigable and relentless bloodhounds, were tracking them down—military police who were ordered to kill them as traitors to mother Russia.

*

Kateryna opened the back door a crack, slowly, holding her father's pistol tightly in her right hand and pointing it toward the ragged specter outside in front of her.

The soldier raised both of his hands above his shoulders. His hands were dirty, grimy; but they were empty. There was a pleading, desperate look in his eyes.

"I won't hurt you," he said in Russian. "We…"

"We?" Kateryna inquired.

"Yes, 'we.'" the soldier replied.

"There are four of us now. We were all in the same T-90 tank when the Javelin hit the tank right in front of ours. It was so powerful that it blew the turret off. The turret almost hit our tank and we were thirty yards behind. All of the soldiers inside were instantly killed including the captain who was our commanding officer. When we saw what happened to the tank in front of us, we thought our tank would be next, so we took off. Initially there were six of us, but our lieutenant and one of those who stayed behind started shooting at us. Two of us were killed and one of us, Matvey, was hit in the arm and was wounded. I am the oldest, a corporal and the others with me are privates. So, I am the leader.

"The military police are pursuing us with their dogs. We are being hunted and there is nowhere to hide except here in the woods. But that provides no shelter. Can you help us? Is there somewhere we can hide here…to get out of the cold and the snow? Please?" he pleaded. "We have nowhere to hide and the military police surely will hunt us down and surely they will kill us."

Kateryna paused, thinking of her family and herself. And thinking of the plight of the young Russian soldier and his three comrades, particularly the wounded one.

Then, after weighing concern for her family's safety and her urge to protect the vulnerable Russians, she pointed toward her father's chicken coop, and said, "Wait over there while I get dressed. Then we can talk further."

*

After getting dressed and putting on her heavy winter coat and cap, Kateryna met the young soldier outside the chicken coop.

"We ran away because your Ukrainian army is destroying our convoy." he began. "The Ukrainians are blowing up our tanks. That was not supposed to happen. Our commanders told us we'd be safe within our tanks . . . that nothing could hurt us . . . and then when we saw what could happen, we knew that what they had told us was a lie. We felt betrayed . . . betrayed by our own leaders. And that was not the only lie they told us. They assured us we'd be welcomed by the Ukrainian people . . . that we'd be freeing them from the Nazis . . . freeing them from persecution and the forces of evil. That, too, was a lie. Instead, it is we who are the forces of evil. It is our leaders . . . the Russian leaders and not the Ukrainian leaders who are the Nazis and I now despise them."

Then he told her his name was Pavel and that he was from a small town in eastern Siberia, Kyzyl. He said it was a small town like Kovpyta, the nearby village where Kateryna was from. He said that he'd been forced to join the Russian army; and, because of his mechanical skills, he had been assigned to the tank corps. He said that all he wanted to do was to stay in his hometown and continue working in his father's auto repair shop which he hoped to inherit someday. But then, the military came into his village and made all of the young men leave their families—in some cases, leave their wives and their small children and join the ranks of the Russian army. He told her that he was lucky that he did not have a wife or any children—only a sister and middle-aged parents.

He told her, with tears welling in his eyes, that when they came west with the army they were not told where they were, only that they were forces of liberation of their fellow countrymen. Then they learned the truth: that they were in Ukraine, that many Ukrainians had relatives in Russia and that many Ukrainians themselves had been born in Russia. And they learned that most of the people they were ordered to kill spoke Russian. And he told her that he was appalled and horrified and terribly ashamed of what he and his comrades had been ordered to do, the atrocities they were forced to commit in Bucha and elsewhere.

Kateryna stood patiently listening, shivering in the cold night air despite her heavy winter coat as Pavel told her this. When he finished, she told him that he and his three comrades could spend the night in her father's barn.

"There's lots of hay in the loft above the cow stalls," she said. "You can sleep there until the morning. Sleeping on the hay may not be very comfortable, but at least it is dry, and it will be warmer than being outside in the cold and the wind.

"In the morning, I will bring some food for you . . . and some warm water and a clean bandage for your comrade's arm."

*

Shortly before dawn as the eastern skies were first beginning to pearl from gray to faint pink, again there was a tap on Kateryna's window. She woke from a deep sleep with a bolt, shook the last of a dream from her head and quickly rolled out of bed. Having anticipated something like this, she'd slept fully dressed.

Barefoot, she went to the back door where she greeted Pavel.

He looked bedraggled and weary but at least he'd had a few hours of sleep on the straw in the hayloft with his companions.

Kateryna looked nervously at the door to her parents' bedroom. She heard nothing from within. Briefly, she thought about inviting Pavel in for coffee but decided against it. *Even if the dog doesn't bark and Papa doesn't wake up, how would I explain the mud he might track in.*

"Wait here," she said. "I'll bring you some things for you to eat and a clean bandage for your comrade's arm."

*

After handing him the items she'd assembled, she smiled, wished him well and turned to go back to her bedroom.

"Wait. Please wait a minute, Miss. I want to thank you. Thank you so very, very much. You are helping to save our lives.

"By the way, I don't know your name."

"My name is Kateryna."

"Thank you, Kateryna." He said earnestly.

Then, as he took one step back, he turned and said, "Oh, and one more thing, may we come again if we need more food and . . ." he paused, and then added "more bandages for Matvey's arm?"

Kateryna thought for a minute. *Why not*, she thought. *We have plenty to give and if we can do so safely, why not?*

"Yes," she replied, "we can continue to help you, but I need to know when you'll be coming so I can have things ready for you."

"How can we arrange that?" he asked.

Kateryna thought for a minute. Then she went back into her bedroom. She returned a few minutes later holding something behind her back.

"Here," she said, handing him the object. "Tie this around that young birch over there at dusk on a night you'll be coming. I'll check the birch each night before I go to bed. If it's there, I will know you'll be coming, and I'll have food and water for you. Bandages too if your comrade needs them. Just tap on my window, I'll get up and help you if I know you're coming. But be very, very careful. And don't tell anyone. No telling what the Russians would do to me or to my family if they found out I was helping you."

Then she handed him the object she was holding behind her back. It was a Ukrainian flag. A blue and yellow flag. Blue for the normally peaceful sky above her country and yellow for the abundant grain her country produces for its people and the people of the world.

It was a small flag, but it was big enough to wrap around the birch tree.

*

From the steps at the backdoor, Kateryna watched Pavel leave as the night slowly dissolved into dawn. He left with six old hens, their necks wrung, and heads severed tied to his waist and a bag full of potatoes and another of freshly hatched eggs. His three companions waited for him, barely visible at the edge of the woods like ephemeral ghosts.

Kateryna watched Pavel trudge across the backyard. When he got to the rim of the trees, he stopped and waved. He also said something which, given the breeze and the distance between them, she could not hear. But, struggling to read his lips once again, she thought he said, "Thank you! Thank you! You are . . ." and she couldn't make out the rest. Had he been closer, she would have heard him say, "You are an angel that God has sent to us!"

He waved once more then melted into the woods disappearing with his comrades.

Kateryna too, waved back. Her lips also moved. It was a prayer of sorts. Had Pavel been close enough to read what her lips said, he would have read, "Good luck and may God bless you and protect you from the dogs and the military police."

9:42 p.m., March 17, 2022
Honchariuske, Ukraine

Kateryna stood on the stoop by the back door looking out into the woods beyond the garden and the field, wondering. It was a quiet evening. All was still except for the occasional haunting call of an owl and the intermittent, silent swooping of swallows darting after gnats in the enveloping darkness.

Scanning the rim of the woods, her eyes settled on the young birch she'd pointed out to Pavel two nights previously. *I wonder if he'll come tonight,* she thought. *It's been two days since I gave him food and that surely wouldn't have lasted very long for four tired and hungry soldiers out in the woods without rations. Perhaps there are others like me who are helping them. And perhaps they've moved on. Or maybe they've been captured. Perhaps even killed. Oh, this terrible, terrible war. When will it stop?*

She looked around. No one from her household was watching. And no lanterns were shining from the neighbors a quarter mile away. So, she thought, *I better go check. No one can see me now. I hope it won't be too early for him to have come, but I don't want to wait any longer. I'm tired and I want to go to bed.*

As she approached the young birch sapling, she thought she heard a rustling deeper in the woods. She stopped and listened hard, tilting her head to the right where the sound had come from.

She heard nothing. *Perhaps it was a rabbit or a racoon,* she thought. But she knew better. A rabbit wouldn't make that much noise. Neither would a racoon.

When she got to the young birch, there it was. The blue and yellow flag tied on a protruding branch of the birch just high enough for her to reach and not low around the trunk where it would have been more visible—visible perhaps to a Russian military police squadron hunting down a band of deserters.

She quickly untied the flag and stuffed it in her blouse.

Then she went back to the farmhouse. She knew she had some gathering to do before retiring for the night.

Before the tap on her window would come.

Probably won't get much sleep tonight.

*

The tap on her window came shortly after 1:30 a.m.

She put on her robe, went to the back door, and handed Pavel the larder she'd assembled. This time she included a loaf of bread she'd specially baked that day in hopes that he'd come that night.

*

Pavel thanked her, smiled, and said, "The military police are getting closer. We heard some random shooting earlier in the day. And then some coordinated rifle shots. They sounded like a firing squad, so we knew they were close and that we had to stay ahead of them.

"So, this will certainly help. My brothers and I must stay well nourished."

"What about water?" Kateryna asked.

"We've got plenty of that. There's a freshwater stream not far from our camp, but vodka? That would help to keep us warm," he said with a wry smile.

Kateryna returned his smile. "Wait here," she said.

Moments later she returned with an unlabeled bottle she had taken from her father's closet. She knew her father would understand—and approve—when she told him in the morning.

10:56 p.m., March 18, 2022
Honchariuske, Ukraine

The tap on Kateryna's window came earlier than she expected. She had just started to doze off when she heard it. In fact, because she was just starting to fall asleep, she wasn't sure if it was real or a dream.

Then it came again, and she quickly rolled out of bed not wanting him to give up and disappear into the night.

*

"I might have missed you," she said when she greeted him at the back door. "I was starting to fall asleep and I wasn't sure the tap on my window was real or a dream."

"I figured something like that might have happened. So, I tapped a couple of times. The second time a bit harder."

"Here," Kateryna said, handing him a bag of eggs, cheese, bread and a jar of borscht.

"Listen," Pavel said after accepting the bags, "today they got quite close. We were lucky they didn't find where we were hiding.

"They found the camp we'd abandoned at daybreak, but they never found us. We were hiding in a thick grove of pines. They were quite dense and provided us with good cover. Besides, there was a reedy swamp between the pines where we were hiding and the solid ground where they were. They'd either have to wade through the swamp or backtrack a half mile to get to us, and that helped protect us.

"We just held our breath . . . and our rifles . . . as they passed. Fortunately, they didn't see or hear us, and we didn't have to shoot. If one of us had even sneezed, it would have been all over for us.

"Anyway, tomorrow they'll be closing in again and we might not be so lucky.

"Is there any chance we could hide out here . . . on your farm; perhaps in the barn? Even in the chicken coop?"

Kateryna hesitated. She wanted to help them, but she didn't want to put her family in jeopardy. Surely, harboring Russian deserters would expose her family and herself to grave danger if the deserters were discovered. If she got caught.

"Come in for a minute," she finally said. "I need to discuss this with my father."

She knew it wouldn't be necessary to consult with her sister. She knew what her sister's opinion would be.

Part One: Short Stories

*

Fedir staggered out of his bedroom in his nightclothes. He wiped sleep crumbs from his eyes, blinked in the lantern light and scowled as he studied Pavel.

Then, turning to Kateryna, he asked, "Is this the Russian deserter you told me about?"

"Yes, Papa, he is the one. He's the one we've been giving food to . . . and some of your vodka as well."

Fedir scrutinized Pavel, looking him up and down. He noticed the clean spot-on Pavel's sleeve where he'd torn off his corporal's stripes. Then he turned to Pavel, nodded his approval, and said, "Ahh . . . my vodka. I hope it helped to keep you warm," giving him a wink.

Kateryna then proceeded to tell her father about Pavel's request.

"Mmmm," Fedir said. "Here, sit down, young man," he said gesturing toward a chair beside the kitchen table. "Let me think. We don't have much to offer. Certainly, you four cannot stay here in our home. That would be much too dangerous for my family. Besides, our home is too small, and it is overcrowded as it is on account of Kateryna, her older sister, Nataliya, and her two youngsters, Dmytro and Svetlana. They fled from their village when the Russians first attacked. And they are living here now with my wife and me on my farm.

"But I'd like to help. There are four of you, as I understand it?"

"Yes, Sir. Four of us, and one is wounded. He was shot in his left arm when we ran from the tank convoy, but he can still fight."

"Ahh . . . that reminds me. There were four of us also when we got separated from our battalion when we were fighting against the Nazis in World War II . . . when we Ukrainians were part of the Russian army. Conscripts we were. Just boys back then. Two of us hadn't even started to shave. We hid in an abandoned home back then in '44. The Germans had bombed it, and it was deserted. The roof and one side were blown away.

"But I don't know of anything like that near here. So, you'd have to get closer to Kyiv in order to find . . ."

"What about our barn, Papa?" Kateryna interjected.

"Mmmm . . ." the old man murmured. "That might work for a short while. Yes, that might work temporarily. At least it would keep them out of the cold."

"And I could give them some hot tea. Oh, and you do have some extra blankets, don't you Papa?"

"Yes, yes. We have some they can use."

"They would be most welcome. Thank you very much. You are very generous," Pavel said.

"We're glad to help you" the old soldier said. "We hate the Russians. What they are doing to our country . . . to our people . . . it is horrible, beyond horrible. It is unforgivable, unpardonable. Not even God could forgive what they are doing. Obliterating towns and cities with their bombs and their missiles. Destroying hospitals and schools. Annihilating our people. Killing our citizens . . . raping our women and killing our children, innocent little babies, for Heaven's sake. And why? What did we do? We did nothing to provoke this . . . incite this war. We are innocent. This invasion is totally unjustified. It is an abomination in the eyes of the Lord. And the acts they are committing are war crimes.

"So, yes. Yes, we will support you. Yes, you may hide in our barn. And if the Russians come and ask if we have seen you . . . even if they ask if you are hiding in our barn, I will tell them 'Go look in the barn if you want to, but do not disturb my cows!'"

"But Papa, what if the Russian soldiers do discover they are here and that we are harboring them?"

"Then we will fight them," Pavel answered without waiting for Fedir to reply. "Even Matvey, our wounded one. We will fight them. We have rifles and ammunition, and we will protect you . . . protect your home and your family and we will kill them."

3:37 p.m., March 20, 2022
Honchariuske, Ukraine

Dmytro was the first to see them. He was out in the backyard kicking a soccer ball between two stones he'd placed against the side of the barn when he saw the squad of Russian military police at the edge of the woods looking intently at his grandparents' home, checking a map and talking amongst themselves. There were six of them.

Dmytro abruptly stopped. He left the soccer ball which he was about to kick and darted toward the backdoor.

The Russian soldiers saw him. One raised his rifle and pointed it at the running boy, but another put out his arm and pulled the rifle down. "Don't shoot," he said. "You probably won't hit the kid and you'll only alert those in the house. They're the ones we want. Not the boy."

When Dmytro got inside, he ran to his mother and blurted breathlessly, "There . . . there are soldiers . . . out . . . out in the woods. In back . . . out in the woods!"

Nataliya, who was braiding Svetlana's hair, stopped, and put down her rat-tail comb. She went to the kitchen window and cautiously pulled back the curtain. She looked out to the backyard and the woods. She immediately saw the Russian military police and she shouted for her father and Kateryna. They quickly came and the three of them looked out at the squadron of military police.

"See, I told you they would come! I told you this was dangerous! That we shouldn't have helped the deserters! Now, we're going to be in for it!" Nataliya, spinning toward her sister and father, her eyes flaring, angrily snarled.

Kateryna and Fedir were silent. They just looked at one another. Finally, Fedir whispered to Kateryna, "Give me a minute. Then I'll go out and talk with them. I'll see if I can get them to go away. I think I have something in my closet that will help. When I am talking with them, you take the milk pail, put on your apron, and go out to the barn pretending you're going to milk the cows and warn our friends. Walk calmly and naturally. Do not run and do not under any circumstances look at the Russians."

*

When Fedir emerged from his bedroom, he was wearing his World War II tunic—his then Russian uniform—over his shirt. It was much too small and ill-fitting. He couldn't button it in front and the sleeves were halfway up to his elbow. But it was Russian, and he thought it might be helpful for what he was about to do.

He went out to the backyard and, in Russian, said, "What do you want? As you can see, I am one of you. I fought in your army our . . . army . . . the Soviet Army . . . against the Nazis many, many years ago. So how can I help you, my comrades?"

The leader of the Russians, the solider who had pushed down his comrade's rifle, replied, "We are looking for deserters. Four of them and we think they may have been here. We think you may have given them food and water. We think you may even be hiding them, old *comrade!*" the squadron leader called back derisively.

"I know nothing of what you are talking about. I feed only my family, my cows, my chickens, my dog, and my cats. I don't know anything about deserters. I myself hated deserters from our army back when I was a Russian soldier like you long . . . before your time."

Just then Kateryna came out of the house wearing her apron and carrying a milk pail. She walked calmly and slowly toward the barn. Perhaps too slowly and with too much apparent calm. She purposefully kept her head rigidly forward so as not to look toward the woods. So as not to look toward the Russian military police.

"Who is she?" the leader shouted to Fedir. "And where is she going?"

"She is my daughter. She lives here with my wife and me. She is going to milk the cows."

"It is midday. It is too early to milk the cows. Besides, your cows are not in the barn. They are out in the pasture over there," the leader said, pointing to a fenced-in field on the far side of the barn.

"But one of my cows is still in the barn. She is sick and not out with the others. That is the cow my daughter is intending to milk."

"You are lying, old man. It is too early in the day to milk any cow. And no one would want milk from a sick cow. And besides, if the sick cow has not been out in the field eating, how can she produce milk? And why is your daughter walking so slowly and stiffly? I think she may be going to warn the deserters. I think the deserters may be hiding in your barn. Let's go, comrades," he barked to his men. As he did so, he raised his rifle toward Kateryna who was nearing the barn door.

"No, no. Don't shoot her. She is innocent," the old soldier, Fedir, shouted.

"'Innocent' you say? Then you are not." the leader replied. As he turned his rifle away from Kateryna and pointed it at Fedir. "You are a liar, and you too are a traitor, old 'comrade.'" Then he fired. Just once. That was all that was required. Fedir staggered backward toward the house then crumpled awkwardly to the ground.

Seeing what had just happened to Fedir, his wife, Oksana, screamed and ran from the house to where her husband lay.

The leader then shot her as well.

*

Kateryna ran safely to the barn. It had a sliding door which Pavel quickly slid open for her. He had been watching from the crack in the door.

"Come in. Hurry. We'll hide you safely behind the cow stalls. I'll get my brothers to protect you."

As he did so, he signaled to his three companions and shouted, "Sasha and Egor, you come down and take up positions here on the ground floor. Matvey, you stay up there by the window. When they come forward, open fire. I'm going to go around to the other side of the house and fire at them from there."

*

Just then, three of the miliary police emerged from the woods; in crouching, hunchbacked runs, they darted toward the farmhouse. It was simple target practice for Sasha and Egor. They quickly fired from the barn door dispatching all three. Only one of their four combined shots missed its target.

"Three down. Three more to go," Egor whispered to Sasha.

Seeing what had just happened to half of his squad, the Russian leader put down his rifle; and, from behind a tree, grabbed a grenade launcher. He sighted the barn door and squeezed the trigger.

The barn door exploded. Egor and Sasha were instantly killed.

Then the leader, seeing a blur behind the barn window, reloaded the grenade launcher, sighted and pulled the trigger a second time. That too was a direct hit. Matvey never knew what hit him.

*

Pavel winced as he heard the grenades explode and guessed what happened. Swallowing hard, he peered around the far corner of the farmhouse and waited. A moment later, he spotted the Russian squad leader conferring with his two remaining comrades.

He carefully raised his rifle, sighted between the leader's shoulder blades, and squeezed the trigger. The leader lurched forward, spewing blood from his mouth, and crumpled to the ground.

The two remaining Russian soldiers—now leaderless—looked at one another and then quickly retreated deep into the woods. The fight was over.

Of the deserters, only Pavel remained.

*

After the skirmish was over, Kateryna emerged from the barn. What she saw sickened her. She had to choke back the bile rising from her stomach. Her father was lying face down twenty feet in front of his back door. Blood was oozing from his back, reddening his old, ill-fitting World War II tunic. He was not moving, and she knew he was gone.

Then there was her mother. She, too, lying face down and hemorrhaging from her neck. Her right hand outstretched, grasping the left leg of her husband.

Kateryna sobbed and could not hold back a flood of tears as she knelt by the bodies of her parents. *Those butchers . . . those monstrous, despicable murderers . . . .*

Soon—and safely after the gunfire ceased—Svetlana, Dmytro, and Nataliya joined her. Dmytro stood silently staring at the bodies of his grandparents. His mouth agape, his lips quivering and his eyes wide and unblinking. Nataliya clung to her mother's knees, sobbing. Svetlana stood rigidly, impassively, her eyes scanning the woods, searching for any remaining Russian soldiers.

"They killed my mother and father!" Kateryna wailed through tears to Pavel as he approached from behind the farmhouse. "But you saved my sister, niece, and nephew. Me as well. And you have killed the Russians. Thank you. Thank you for that. But . . . oh . . . oh . . . my parents. Why did they have to shoot them? My father my . . . father as he said . . . was once one of them. But I am glad that you killed them all. They all deserved to . . ."

"Not all of them, I'm afraid," Pavel replied, "we only killed four. Two of them escaped. Presumably, they will go back to their company. They retreated into the woods after their leader went down and I couldn't get a shot off at them.

"But now you must leave. It is not safe here any longer. Those two who escaped will tell their commanding officers when they get back to our . . . I mean 'their' . . . main encampment. It is no longer my encampment. It is no longer my company.

"They will report what happened here. And their commanders will insist on retaliation . . . on revenge. They will send out another squadron to capture or kill you . . . all of you and to capture or kill me. So, you must flee . . . we all must flee.

"I saw what my countrymen did in Bucha when our convoy got stalled there. Saw the horrible crimes they committed with my own eyes. Saw the atrocities. They were butchers in Bucha!

"They captured several men who'd stayed behind, tortured them, then tied their hands behind their backs and shot them in the head. They left them in a ditch to rot. Meanwhile, they raped their wives and sisters. They even stole their chickens' chickens like yours . . . plucked them and roasted them in the backyards of their victims' homes while their bodies lay just yards away.

"And they will do that here as well. So, you must flee. You must go immediately. You must not wait."

"But my parents. They killed them. What about a funeral for them? I must tell our parish priest."

"No, no. There is no time for that now. I will help you bury them out there in the woods or in the barnyard. We can mark their graves with stones. Two for your father and one for your mother or however you wish. That way, you will know which grave is which if you ever return."

"I will return," Kateryna replied resolutely.

"But then we must leave. Immediately afterward we must leave. Your sister can help us. Just take your identification papers and what money you have. Then we must go. All of us. The military police or the soldiers will return, and they will rape you and your sister, then kill us all. Even the children. So, we must hurry."

"Are there shovels in the barn?"

"Yes, there is a shovel and a spade and a hoe. Svetlana, show Pavel where they are."

*

After burying her parents and marking their shallow graves with stones, Kateryna stood for a moment, bowed her head and said in Ukrainian, "Please, Lord, receive these our parents and grandparents into your eternal embrace and love."

Dmytro and Nataliya stood, heads also bowed, at Kateryna's side, each holding a hand of their aunt. Sevtlana shifted from foot to foot behind them, looking nervously into the woods.

Pavel stood in respectful silence to the side. When he saw that Kateryna had raised her head, he stepped forward, tapped her on the shoulder and said, "Come now. It is time for us to leave. The military police will soon be here."

*

Two days later, after spending the night in the deserted shell of a bombed-out home on the outskirts of Kyiv, they arrived at the train depot, Kyiv-Parazynski, in Kyiv. They were tired. They were hungry. And they were desperate.

But they were safe.

10:56 a.m., March 22
Kyiv-Parazynski Train Station, Kyiv, Ukraine

The train to Lviv finally arrived at 10:56 a.m. It had been scheduled to depart at 9:30 but airstrikes the day before on the outskirts of Kyiv had damaged the tracks to Lviv. After extraordinary efforts, emergency repairs were completed, and trains were ready to roll once again.

While repairs to the tracks were being made, anxious passengers huddled on the platform. Many had stayed through the night. Mothers comforting wailing and sobbing children. Old women with glassy eyes—most of them wearing scarfs tied around their heads—staring into the distance, silently lamenting the forced departure from their homes and towns. Apprehensive and uncertain as to their future. Not knowing their destination. Fearful it would be in a country whose language they would not understand, whose customs and cultures would be strange and bewildering, and whose laws and edicts might be harsh and punitive.

*

After hours of waiting and frequent but unrewarded scanning of the empty tracks, at last a train—at first a spectral dot on the horizon—emerged out of the distance, grew, came steadily on and finally rumbled to a stop beside the platform. It hissed and shook for a moment and then its doors sluiced open.

The women and children and what few men there were—all of them elderly and well past fighting age—somberly got on board.

It was an orderly process, not a mad, hectic scramble to get on like scenes of some other evacuations. This one was joyless, somber, and fatalistic. Sadness and apprehension prevailed. Women grieved at leaving their husbands, sons, brothers, fathers, and grandfathers behind. They were pensive and uncertain as to their future, where they would end up, whether they'd ever return, whether they'd ever see their loved ones or their homes again.

*

Nataliya, Dimytrea, and Svetlana were among those who'd boarded the train. As he stepped on board, Dmytro turned and waved to Kateryna, who remained on the platform. Following her older brother's example, Nataliya did the same. Svetlana, however, did not. She'd given her sister a perfunctory hug, a peck on the cheek, but she did not look back or wave when she stepped onto the train.

Meanwhile, Kateryna remained on the platform. Pavel stood close in front of her. She looked deep into his eyes. She was holding both of his hands, and she was crying.

"How can I ever thank you?" she whispered.

He smiled, then bent forward and kissed her right cheek. With that, Kateryna flung herself into his arms. They clung to one another for nearly a minute as the platform emptied and most of the passengers stepped on board.

"You must get on the train now," Pavel said. "We have come a long distance and endured many hardships to get here. I don't want you to miss this opportunity to get away."

As they held one another close, Pavel looked from side to side warily. There were several Ukrainian policemen milling about. He knew that a Russian soldier standing at the train station in Kyiv—even one with his regimental insignia badge and corporal's stripes ripped from his sleeve—surely would attract attention. *At least they won't think I'm a fifth columnist,* he thought. *A fifth columnist would not be wearing a Russian uniform out here on this platform.*

"Will I ever see you again?" Kateryna asked, fearful of his answer, but knowing what it most certainly would be.

Their eyes met.

"I do not know," he said, "but I will try. After this war is over, I will return to Kovpyta where you were a teacher, and I will look for you. But now I must go into hiding. I will see if I can join the Ukrainian forces and fight against my former comrades . . . the invaders. Hopefully, they will accept me . . . take me in. I could be valuable to them because there is much that I know about them. Besides, I am a good soldier. I shoot very accurately.

"But now you must go. You must go now." he said once again. "Before the train is filled with refugees. It will be leaving soon. You must get on it right away."

Kateryna leaned forward and kissed him. Kissed him hard on the lips, then looked deep into his eyes again. After yet a long moment of clinging to him, she turned and without saying anything more, stepped from the platform onto the train. There, she paused, looked back and waved. He, too, paused, looked longingly and wistfully at her, then anxiously and fearfully glanced over his shoulder at the group of onlookers standing behind the platform. Particularly at the men in uniform standing there.

*

On board the train, Kateryna pushed her way to a window. She desperately wanted to wave to Pavel one more time before the train pulled away from the station.

That's when she saw two Ukrainian policemen seize Pavel by his armpits and lead him off. A third marched behind with a pistol raised in his hand.

She never got to wave a final goodbye.

THE CONFESSION OF OBERLEUTNANT HELMUT PRAHL

Oberleutnant Helmut Prahl paused on the steps of the cathedral of St. Viktor in Xanten, Germany. He was home on leave from the 4th Army under the command of Field Marshal Ernst Busch. In June of 1941, the German Wehrmacht had captured most of Lithuania, including the city of Kowno.

It wasn't the bright sunny Saturday afternoon that made Oberleutnant Prahl pause on the steps before entering the semidarkness of the cathedral; it was what he had witnessed in Kowno on August 10, 1941, that made him pause.

For several weeks, he had agonized as to what he should do. Should he confess to what he had seen? Would that be a treasonous act against the German army, against the Fatherland? Even against the Führer himself? After all, his commanding officers had made it quite clear that the real enemies of the Third Reich were Jews and Bolsheviks. That they were the ones who had fomented the war. That they were the ones who had made it "necessary" for the Wehrmacht and the Luftwaffe to attack the Baltics. That they were an existential threat to Germany. And that they had to be exterminated. That's what he had been told. And that's what many of his fellow officers and many of those under his command genuinely believed.

But he knew better. He knew that what he'd witnessed violated every principle that his church stood for. He knew that what he'd seen was an atrocity beyond all things imaginable. And yet it had been real. He had seen it. He had observed an unspeakable horror. And he had just stood by and watched. He had taken no action to prevent it. He hadn't spoken out. He hadn't uttered a single word or lifted even a finger in opposition or protest. He'd simply stood by and watched.

Was he guilty for not having prevented it? He could have easily ordered those under his command to stop it. But he knew if he did, he'd be subject to discipline. Perhaps even sentenced to one of the camps. One of the camps from which those who entered rarely came out. Came out alive, that is.

There were even reports from some of his fellow officers—oberleutnants like himself—that higher-ranking Wehrmacht commanders were collaborating with the SS. Reports of the mass firing squads, liquidations of the evil Jews and troublesome Bolsheviks. Firing squads and liquidations in which the army participated. Shootings of citizens by soldiers. The slaughter of innocents. At first just men, but eventually even women and children. He knew these were war crimes. More fundamentally, he knew it was morally wrong. Horribly, horribly morally wrong. And what he had seen, too, was horribly, horribly wrong. Yet he had done nothing to stop it.

He had heard that the shootings were ordered by Himmler and Heydrich. And he knew from whom they had received their endorsements, their orders, their encouragement. And he knew that many German citizens, "good citizens" as they were known, supported these shootings, these liquidations. "Good German citizens" who believed what their Führer told them was right. After all, he was their leader.

He had even seen stick-figure drawings taken home from his nephew's school, young children's depictions of firing squads shooting Jews. Hateful portrayals of atrocities commissioned by antisemitic schoolmasters.

But he knew it all was wrong. Terribly, terribly wrong. Against every moral code that he—a former altar boy—had ever been taught. Against the words of Christ. Against God's law. And he knew too that if the reports he had heard were true—that Wehrmacht officers were condoning terror and atrocities under the direct orders of Himmler, Heydrich and the Führer himself—then surely there'd be reprisals against him if he sought to intervene. Perhaps he'd even be shackled and blindfolded and stood up with his back against a wall.

So Oberleutnant Helmut Prahl hesitated on the cathedral steps. He looked down at the sheen glistening on his boots. Then he crossed himself, pushed open the heavy oak door, and went in.

*

Oberleutnant Helmut Prahl made the sign of the cross once again as he sat behind the screen that separated him from the priest on the other side.

"Bless me, Father, for I have sinned. My last confession was several months ago. Just before I went to the front with the 4th Army of our

Wehrmacht. I am an oberleutnant serving under Field Marshal Busch. I was the commander of 36 men in my unit. On August 10, we were in the central square at Kowno to the east of Vilnius in Lithuania. It was approximately 15:00 hours on Sunday afternoon. The city's police had rounded up around 50 Jews. The police circled them with guns drawn should any bolt and try to escape.

"A local townsman, a big fellow, six foot three or four, stepped forward carrying a club. He had rusty red hair and was wearing coveralls. He gestured to the policemen and called for them to push one of the Jews toward him. A policeman stood behind one of the Jews, his pistol shoved in the Jew's back and marched him forward. When the Jew got within a meter of the townsman, the townsman swung the club striking the Jew on his left ear. The Jew crumpled and fell face-down in the public square. The townsman then proceeded to beat him unmercifully. Blood poured from the Jew's mouth, nose and from his ears.

"When the townsman was satisfied, he'd killed the Jew, he beckoned for the police to send him another. And then another. And another.

"And so it went until all of the Jews had been clubbed to death.

"All the while, the assembled onlookers cheered and applauded as each Jew was brought forward and slaughtered. Some women in the crowd even held their young children up so they could get a better view.

"My soldiers stood by passively and watched. Some even took photographs. No one intervened to stop the massacre. I, too, Father, took no steps to stop the slaughter. I could have done so, but I didn't.

"Then the townsman and the police piled all the corpses in a heap and the townsman climbed on top of the dead Jews. This time he wasn't holding his club. This time he held an accordion which he started to play. It was *Tautiška giesmethė*, the Lithuanian national anthem.

"It was an atrocity, Father, a horrible, horrible atrocity. I cannot banish the horror from my mind. Cannot banish it from my dreams.

"Am I guilty of a sin, Father? Can I ever gain absolution?"

The priest hearing confessions that afternoon was an old man in his eighties. He had nominally retired and only rarely was he called upon to preside over Mass. But he did hear confessions, especially on Saturdays.

He'd heard all sorts of confessions over the course of his fifty-plus years of ministry. Confessions of infidelity, greed, theft—even rape and murder. But he had never heard anything like Oberleutnant Helmut Prahl's confession. Accordingly, thoughtful priest that he was, he paused, searching for the right words, the right thoughts, silently praying he'd receive some guidance from above.

Oberleutnant Helmut Prahl shifted nervously on the confessional bench. Tiny drops of sweat formed on his forehead. One droplet fell on his right boot staining the shine.

Oberleutnant Prahl awaited the priest's pronouncement.

Finally, Father Walther Rhees nodded once, then responded to the penitent on the other side of the screen.

"My Son, what you witnessed was indeed horrible and despicable. A terrible act beyond all forgiveness and absolution. The actions of the Lithuanian townsman were acts that God Himself cannot and will not forgive. So, too, those of the assembled townsfolk and police who stood and watched and cheered. Those, too, were deplorable, abominable, and unforgiveable acts.

"And the words of our leaders depicting Jews as evil, as a treacherous, sinister force that caused this war, those are wrongs as well. And the fact that they were uttered by those at the highest levels of our government does not make them legitimate. In fact, it only makes them even more contemptible, more damnable. Some in the priesthood have spoken out against what our leaders have said and continue to say. Indeed, some of them have been arrested for speaking out. But we shall continue to do so. We must do so because those words which our country's leaders speak and the actions taken in response to their words offend the teachings of Our Lord and Savior Jesus Christ.

"But your actions . . . rather, your inaction . . . your failure to intervene . . . I cannot condemn as sinful. Had you taken steps to prevent the wrongs and atrocities you saw, you would have subjected yourself and those under your command to punishment. Perhaps you even would have suffered death. I have heard that such things occur in these times. So not only you, but perhaps the soldiers under your command might have been shot as traitors had you intervened.

"Therefore, you committed no sin. Your heart and your thoughts were innocent, free from guilt. Inaction in this case was not a sin. The horror and revulsion you felt and continue to feel is evidence of your innocence. And it is also punishment for any guilt you may think you have.

"As for our leaders who make speeches encouraging such atrocities . . . especially those who command such atrocities . . . their time of judgment will come. The Lord God will hold them accountable and pass judgment upon their souls. We can only hope that He will bring this war and these atrocities to an end. And that He will do so soon.

"In the meantime, we . . . we in the Church must continue to speak out. From the pulpit, we must condemn the wrongs committed by our countrymen. Especially those of our leaders.

"So, my son, by the power Jesus Christ has conferred to me to grant the remission of sins, I absolve you in the name of the Father and of the Son and of the Holy Spirit from any transgression arising out of your passivity and inaction that afternoon in Kowno.

"I cannot predict the outcome of this war. I cannot assume that the Church's words will change the conduct and the words of our leaders. I can only pray for the salvation of you and all Germans…including those who are tempted to follow Satan. And as it is my duty to my Lord Jesus Christ, I shall pray for our leaders. I shall pray for their souls. And I shall pray that all the people of our country and all the people of Europe and the greater world will be spared from such atrocities. But I fear that prayers alone will not be enough.

"I fear that such depravity lies deep within the hearts of many in mankind. And I fear that as in the time of Sodom and Gomorrah, God's wrath and vengeance will fall upon mankind.

"And so, my son, your confession has motivated me to speak out. To speak out against this evil infecting our country. And I shall ask the senior pastor of the cathedral who succeeded me to allow me to speak from the pulpit tomorrow at our masses. To speak out against and condemn all such atrocities."

*

The day after hearing Oberleutnant Helmut Prahl's confession, the old priest did speak out. With an unquavering voice belying his years, he forcefully condemned the acts of violence and atrocities the Nazis were committing against the Jews and other innocents.

Four days later he was seized by the Gestapo.

The day after that he was tortured. And for five subsequent days he was tortured.

Then—on the seventh day—he was led out, shackled, and made to stand against a wall. A wall with many pock marks.

That is where he was shot.

TWO SETS OF HANDS

Kyiv-Parazynski
The Train Station in Kyiv, Ukraine
March 2022

The little girl (we'll call her Svetlana) pressed the palm of her left hand hard against the window of the train. From the inside. She was looking out at the man standing on the platform outside. Sadly. Imploringly. Tears bulging in her eyes and streaming down her cheeks.

The man on the platform was her father. He, too, was pressing his hand hard against the window. Hard against the glass. The outside of the window.

It was his right hand, and it dwarfed her tiny left. Their fingers yearned to entwine. It might be for the last time. But the glass intervened, and their hands could not touch. They kept their hands in place as long as they could, but their fingers could not join.

Then the train lurched, moved forward a few feet, paused, then surged again and was off.

*

"Daddy, Daddy, please, please come with us," Svetlana cried out to the diminishing figure on the platform.

*

The father (we'll call him Yurii) stood at the edge of the platform for a long time. Well after the train turned a bend and was out of sight.

Yurii was a soldier in the Ukrainian army. A sergeant. His squadron stood behind him in front of the terminal. None of the men spoke. They just let their leader have his moment.

*

Will I ever see her again? Yurii thought.

*

After a minute or so, Yurii, out of the corner of his eye, saw one of his men shifting from foot to foot. He knew he must take charge. He knew he must take command. But even though the train was out of sight, he cast one last lingering look down the empty tracks.

Tears, too, welled in his eyes. He didn't want his men to see them. So he blinked several times, bowed his head and shook them away.

Finally, he turned and said, "Well, let's go."

He hoped his men hadn't noticed the two salty rivulets drying on his cheeks.

PART TWO:
STORY-POEMS

RAIN

I.

They came from the same roots, Fareed and Ravil did. The same neighborhood. The same streets. The same schools. And most of all, the same church. And they worshiped and prayed together. As did their wives and children. For years. Side by side. Literally, side by side.

But in their thirties, their views began to diverge. It started when a visiting church leader form outside their district came to their church and talked about the need to expand the meaning of the church's foundational principles, to reinterpret them in light of the modern world, the world of technology, commerce, global travel and progress.

The leaders of the church were appalled by what he said. They asserted just the opposite. That the values and principles of the outside world, the world of computers, the internet and social media were lax, debasing, corrupting, the works of the devil; and, in a single word: immoral. They argued the need to adhere even more steadfastly to the church's orthodox rules. "To return to our heritage. To be true to our traditional beliefs and practices," as they summed it up, "for these beliefs and practices have served us well for centuries and will continue to serve us well in these times of challenge from the outside world."

Ravil agreed with the elders of the church.

Part Two: Story-Poems

Fareed wasn't so sure. To him, the message of the outsider rang true, put into words many of the ideas he felt stirring within him, that he intuitively felt, but was unable to articulate. But when he heard the outsider speak, those vaguely formed, amoebic stirrings within, took immediate shape, were clear and defined. They resonated and he knew that they were true and right. And he knew that the outsider's words were what he wanted for his wife and more importantly, for his children. Particularly for his daughters.

True, many of the points made by the outsider dealt with what at first seemed like minor matters. Things like what women should be permitted to wear, what they could do for the church, reading material appropriate for children—things like that. But, as sometimes happens, little things grew to be big—as acorns turn into giant oaks—and as a seed once planted . . . .

So, Fareed began to read and study further the subjects that the outsider had talked about. And he found other sources, other texts and other tracts which spoke of these new directions, and which departed even further from the orthodox tenets adhered to by the elders. And he obtained tapes of sermons along similar lines which he asked to have played in the sanctuary of the church; and, if not there, then in the basement where sometimes more informal meetings were held.

But the elders of the church were opposed. So was Ravil. Indeed, Ravil was quite upset by Fareed's proposals. He was so offended that he forbade his wife to speak with Fareed's wife and forbad his children to play with Fareed's. The families no longer worshipped together; and, eventually, Ravil stopped talking to Fareed altogether.

But that was months ago.

That was before Fareed opened a new school—albeit a very small one, but a new school nevertheless—in an empty storefront two blocks away from the church. That was before Fareed started hiring teachers from other districts who believed in the new ideas and who began teaching them to those neighborhood children who enrolled in the new school. That was before the children of the new school started communicating these ideas to their friends who attended the older, established school—the school supported by the elders of the church—the school in which Ravil's children were enrolled. And that was before Ravil's children started talking about the new ideas which they had learned from their friends at dinner with Ravil and his wife. Before his children started asking Ravil questions that challenged his beliefs. Challenged what he had always been taught. Challenged his faith.

*

They waited in the basement of the church for the last of the prisoners, Fareed, to arrive. The others had already been captured and were safely secured with their hands and feet taped and tape across their mouths. They were seated on the floor separately so they couldn't touch one another.

The tape, of course, didn't cover the noses of the prisoners and didn't cover their eyes. It didn't hide their furtive, fearful glances, the terror that each one felt.

The guards walked around the prisoners with their guns in the basement of the church. There were twelve guards. Two for each prisoner. They'd gone—six teams of two—to the homes of the prisoners and captured them. Just after ten in the evening. Just before bedtime. Except in the case of one who'd already gone to bed. They interrupted his wife and him and yanked him from their bed. He was the one without a shirt. Just jeans and sandals. And now the tape covering his mouth.

Outside, it was a cloudy night and there was lightning off the distance—out over the sea. And thunder. Soon it would start to rain, one of the guards said. He expressed the wish that they conclude their business before it started to rain. Before the thunder and lightning came. He said he was afraid of lightning. One of the other guards told him to be quiet.

After that, the guards walked around the prisoners with their rifles and their boots and said very little. The only sounds now were the heavy tread of the guards' boots on the basement floor, the strained breathing of the prisoners and the distant thunder.

Like the prisoners, the guards, too, were nervous and scared. Most of them were still boys in their late teens. Only three or four were in their 20s. None was yet 25. Earlier, one of the youngest ones had asked if they really had to do this. An older one assured him that they did. "It is God's will," he said. "Ravil has said so. They have undermined the teachings of the church. They have betrayed the faith. We are the *takfiri,* the true believers, the defenders, and the enforcers of the faith. They are apostates and have forsaken the sacred ways. For this they must be punished. We cannot let them spread their evil creed. Ravil has said it is God's will and that we must do so," he said.

The boy who had asked didn't answer. He looked down. He was afraid the other guards might think that he was weak, might see his tears.

Finally, Ravil came in with Fareed. Fareed was bleeding from a gash on his forehead. His hair and his clothes were disheveled. He'd obviously been beaten. He, too, had his hands taped behind his back and there was tape across his mouth. But not his feet. That enabled him to walk; walk, prodded by a rifle barrel.

Ravil apologized for being late. He said that Fareed had put up a fight—quite a struggle—and that he was glad Nuri and Mamoon had been with him so that they, the three of them, could subdue Fareed.

"Okay. Let's go. Let's take them outside," Ravil said.

The guards cut the tape from the ankles of the other prisoners and prodded them with their guns to get them up. They marched the prisoners up the concrete stairs and out the back door of their church. Some of the prisoners walked forward, erect, defiant. Proud. Fareed was one of those. Others sagged and fell on the steps and had to be kicked and jabbed hard with the rifles to get them to move.

When they were all outside, Ravil ordered the prisoners to be lined up against the wall at the rear of the courtyard behind the church. The guards stepped back away from the prisoners and Ravil began to berate them. He called them traitors and dogs and unbelievers. Fareed's eyes were riveted on Ravil as he spoke. His stare was hard, contemptuous, and unrelenting. For most people, it would have been unsettling. But not for Ravil. It made no impact on Ravil whatsoever. He simply kept berating the prisoners and particularly Fareed for initiating all of the radical and immoral ideas that he and the other apostates had spread—particularly in the new school. Insidious, treacherous ideas that had infected the children—even his own children. He called the prisoners scum for having betrayed the true faith and offended God with their impure ways. And for that, they had to be punished. That is when he ordered them to be shot.

*

Their bodies jumped as the bullets hit them. Afterwards, when they lay slumped on the stones of the courtyard, some of them still twitched and made little jerking motions as if they were trying to awaken. Blood and bits of flesh and bone and other matter had spattered on the wall. The fresh pock marks made by the bullets in the old stone wall shown like newly minted, tiny little silver stars in the spectral lunar light. Little rivers seeped from their wounds, pooled and glistened on the stones in the moonlight. Reflecting the lightning.

Off in the distance, there was thunder.

The boy who had asked if they had to do what now had been done cried softly to himself. His tears made rivulets—little streams—down his dusky, unwashed cheeks. Once again, he hung his head so his tears and his weakness would not be seen.

Ravil then ordered his men to put the bodies into bags, to load the bags with stones and to take them out to sea and dispose of them. The men did as they were told. Silently. The only sound was the squeaking of the swollen plastic bags as they were filled and tied. That and the distant thunder out over the sea. The anthem of the thunder out over sea.

II.

Softly

In the darkest hours

When all was still

And the city slept

When the lights were off

And the traffic gone

While dogs and birds were dreaming

The rain began to fall

Gently

At first just misting

Like a gauze settling

Like moonlight

Slowly lowering itself

Weary and spent

From a long journey

Glistening

Refracting the lunar light

Lambent on the stones

And it was caressing

Caressing and delicate

Tender like a mother's touch

Feeling with blind fingers

Reading the braille

The inscriptions of the braille

The braille upon the pavement

Part Two: Story-Poems

The braille upon the wall
The residue of the prisoners
Their dried blood
Their bits of flesh and bone
Splattered on the wall
Their braille upon the wall
Their braille upon the pavement
The detritus of prisoners
Dried
Splattered
Clinging to the stones
Clinging to the pavement
Clinging to the wall
Then, as if offended,
The rain increased its force
Began to come on stronger
Began to come on hard
Began to fall with vengeance
Pounding down
Beating down
Coming down in torrents
Coming down in waves
Sheets
Sheets of heavy rain
Washing
Rinsing

Until the street was clean
Until the blood was gone
Until the gore was gone
The wall and pavement clean
Clean, no longer stained
And once again the courtyard fresh
Fresh and pure and clean
The courtyard and the air
The air just after rain
Fresh and clean and pure
Reborn
Reborn and fresh again
The gift of cleansing rain
And then the sun arose
Turning dark to gray
In the freshness of the air
The reborn air
The sun set forth the day
Casting forth its light
Its rays
But with the rays came shadows
Shadows on the pavement
Shadows on the stones
Shadows on the courtyard
Shadows on the wall
Shadows of the church

Part Two: Story-Poems

Shadows of its dome
Falling on the pavement
Falling on the stones
Falling on the courtyard
Falling on the wall
Shadows of the church
Shadows that the rain
Could not wash away.

GRACIE

I. January 1956

Gracie rounded 5th and headed north up Ocean Drive. It was her usual route and nearly her usual time. Just a little later this morning because she wanted the sun to be a little higher, the day to be a little warmer.

She had previously noticed that two of the other girls had taken to wearing bikini tops (with no intention of going to the beach) and Gracie decided she'd try it too. *What the heck. I've got the figure,* she thought. *Better than those two I saw out there yesterday.* And indeed, she did.

So, Gracie put hers on. With her short shorts, a scarf around her neck, large circular earrings and oversized sunglasses. A statement worthy of *South Beach,* the local tourist publication guide.

As for her shoes, she paused. The high-top Keds with fresh white socks were stunning with her tan, much more practical, but so mainland, so college girl. Who wanted that? She chose instead her silver high heels, open-toed. *Let 'em see my nails as well*, she thought.

She was headed for the Bus Stop Café at the corner of Ocean and 8th. It had just opened and had a pay phone outside on the 8th Street side. She'd promised her mother in Duluth that she'd call before 11:00 (10:00 her mother's time) and Gracie didn't want to be late. She only had a quarter with her and she hoped the man at the newsstand would exchange it for five nickels. At three minutes apiece, five nickels would be long enough. She wanted to hear what her mother knew about her brother, Ron, who was in Korea at the time. The negotiations at Pammunjon weren't going well, but there was hope nevertheless that Ron and his unit would soon be home from the war. It was now 10:45 and fifteen minutes would have been plenty of time if she'd worn her Keds. But with her heels, she knew she'd have to step it off more briskly than usual. She knew her mother was very punctual—too punctual as far as Gracie was concerned.

Across the street, on the Atlantic side, there were two older men—probably in their 50s or early 60s—sitting on a park bench. Out of the corner of her eye, Gracie saw them elbow each other and lean their heads together, whispering. Gracie stared purposefully forward but she knew they'd seen her. And she knew that they weren't whispering about the weather, basketball scores, or the flea powder they used for their dogs. Even though they were older men, they were men. And their whispering made her proud nevertheless.

At the corner of 6th, three young construction workers were taking a coffee break. One was sitting on the trunk of an Edsel. The other two were standing with their backs to Gracie as she came up Ocean. The one who was seated gestured with a nod of his head and the other two turned toward Gracie. The one closest to her said, "Hey, Babe, how's it goin'! Would ya like a doughnut?"

Gracie strode on past and made no response. Didn't turn her head.

Boys, mere boys, Gracie thought. She liked her men a little older, preferably in their 30s. And at least 25. But, as with the older gentlemen across the street, it was nice to have even the "boys" check her out. Gracie liked the feel of men's eyes no matter what age they were.

In the middle of the 700 block, a blue Nash went past with the windows rolled down. One of the boys inside stuck his head out, whistled, and made a lewd remark. As with the others, Gracie ignored him. Paid him no heed.

At the corner of 8th, she paused on the curb waiting for two younger girls on roller skates to pass. She cast them a critical eye. *Children,* she thought. *What do they know. God, I'm glad I'm past that stage.*

A breeze off the Atlantic caught some strands of her hair and twirled them gently, caressingly, on her bare shoulders. The sun was warm, lotion-like, laving her skin. Where the sun touched, she gleamed like burnished gold; and where it didn't reach, there were shadows, soft, inviting shadows.

After the younger girls passed, Gracie adjusted her sunglasses and started across the street.

When she got to the Bus Stop Café, the man selling papers only had three nickels and a dime to exchange for her quarter. She knew he was telling the truth because he obviously wanted to please her. It was all he could do and required his maximum concentration to count out her change, to avoid staring at her contours.

Three nickels . . . nine minutes . . . that will have to do, Gracie thought.

So, she called her mom and got right through. The operator was very nice. Gracie thought that it might be Hazel, the one who lived two streets over from her parents' home; but she hesitated and didn't ask, and her mother soon was on the party line. Gracie knew that it was important to recognize who the operator was because most of them listened in on calls when they didn't have something else to do. Especially if they knew the callers and the callers were their neighbors.

"Hello, Mom."

"Oh, it's you . . . ."

There was a long pause. Gracie was troubled and concerned.

"Is something wrong?" she said after waiting several seconds. "Is Ron, okay?"

"Yes, Ron's okay . . . ."

And then another pause.

"But something's wrong. I can tell from your voice . . . your hesitation."

"I think that you should know."

Another pause.

"Know what, Mom? Please. Tell me, what's wrong?"

"The photographs."

"What photographs?"

"You know very well what photographs."

"No. No, I don't. What photographs? What are you talking about?"

"In that magazine. Your father's seen them. The whole town's seen them. Even people from the church have seen them. Everyone but me. I refused to look. Your father's mortified. Your grandparents too. They don't even want to leave their house. The whole town's talking about them. There's snickering behind our backs everywhere we go. At work . . . the grocery store . . . your dad . . . ." Her voice trailed off. "I don't even want to talk about it on this party line. You know . . . someone might be listening in."

Again, there was silence. Gracie tried to figure out what her mother was talking about. *What magazine?* She asked herself. She didn't know about any magazine. Then she remembered. *Oh. Oh, my God!* she thought. *Those photographs!*

"Mom, they told me those photos would be strictly private . . . that they'd never be made public. Never be published."

Her mother did not answer.

"Mom, that was months ago when those were taken. And I didn't know they were going to put them in a magazine! They told me it was just for private use . . . that they'd be discreet. They promised . . . and it was just from the waist up. I had my shorts on. With some of the other girls, it was a full exposure . . . ."

"How could you, Gracie? We brought you up so well. We always took you to church. Think of what you've done to your family."

"But, Mom, they promised it was just for something private . . . they promised . . . and I needed the money. Badly. They gave me two hundred bucks, Mom. Cash. Right there on the spot. Two hundred bucks!"

"Well, that may be, but it hardly matters! To let yourself be photographed like that! And in that magazine! You ought to be ashamed!"

"Mom, I needed the money."

"Well, did you at least put it in the bank . . . add it to your savings account?"

"No, Mom. As I've said before, I don't have a savings account."

"Well, do you have the two hundred now?"

Part Two: Story-Poems

"No, Mom. I had to get some things. You know, a purse, some shoes, a bracelet and some
 other things. Clothes, stuff like that. It's important for interviews. But I do have some for my next rent . . . two weeks' worth. By then, I'm sure I'll have a job."

"Gracie, I've got to go. Your father has forbidden me to talk to you and he'll be back any minute now. And I don't want to talk about any of this on an open line."

Another pause ensued.

"You can't call us anymore. You can't call home anymore, Gracie. Goodbye, Gracie." And Gracie heard a click.

*

At six minutes after 11:00, she saw Angelo's red Corvette coming up Ocean and glide into an open parking spot. It was last year's model. A rather daring break from the Corvettes first produced in 1952. They said the 55s were even better sellers than the 52s, the 53s and the 54s. Gracie wasn't so sure. She preferred the earlier models, but times change, and car models had to change too. At least that's what everyone said.

Gracie knew she couldn't keep Angelo waiting. Angelo was an impatient man. He was tall, broad-shouldered, and overweight. 240 or 250. His eyes were deep-set and sinister and he had a large aquiline nose that made him look somewhat like a hawk—somewhat like a predator. Gracie was afraid of him and did not like him but he had what she wanted. What she now knew she needed.

She had to meet him on the beach and not on the sidewalk where they could easily be seen. And she had to do so quickly. Angelo wasn't one to fool around with. He didn't make jokes or small talk. He always got right to the point. You produced the money—the last time it was more than he said it would be—then he produced the goods.

She craved what Angelo sold. It made her feel so good. The first three hits were like golden sunshine filled with honey. They made her feel so good—so warm—so pure.

She knew she needed Angelo.

She needed her next fix.

Part Two: Story-Poems

II. January 2006

Gracie rounded 5th and headed north up Ocean Drive. It was her usual route and nearly her usual time. Just a little bit later this morning because she wanted the sun to be a little higher, the day to be a little warmer.

Across the street, on the Atlantic side, she saw a newspaper lying on the ground beneath a park bench. Gracie liked looking through newspapers. Sometimes there were coupons for free fries or cokes at fast food joints. So she crossed the street to check this edition out. She sat on the bench and picked up the paper. It was yesterday's—January 26, 2006—and the headlines read "Alito Confirmed By Senate." Gracie carefully turned each page but couldn't find anything of value for her. Just some come-on, promise ads for small appliances if you bought a new, flat screen, HD TV. Who had that kind of money? For a new HD TV? Not Gracie. Gracie didn't even have electricity.

She did have a new place, however. And this time, it was even a house. An abandoned home on Collins Avenue, number 909. In its day, it might have been quite nice, but now it was shambles—just right for Gracie.

There was a small courtyard out front. The lawn had long since disappeared, replaced by hardened dirt, bits of broken glass, tiles— the refuse of urban streets. The front door stood ajar. All the windows broken. Some still with remnant, jagged panes. Inside, more trash and broken walls—an iron grated railing on a stairway leading nowhere. Plastic sheeting hanging from a door jamb in the back, flapping with each breeze. A pungent, lingering urine smell.

A faded real estate sign hung out front. "Charles Benson Realty Associates." And across the street, an apartment house. "The Stardust Apartments." And next to that, the "Devine Cyber Lounge and Café."

Gracie was thrilled with her new quarters. For several weeks, she'd bedded down behind the City National branch at the corner of Collins and 5th. She'd found a nice spot behind a dumpster. Her front yard was a parking lot. It was cozy enough. There was a stairwell that no one used, under which Gracie tucked a mattress someone had discarded. Her little den. For shelter and privacy, and she had a cardboard box. One of those refrigerators and large appliances came in. That provided protection from the elements. She even had an outdoor sculpture of sorts, a burnt-out motorcycle standing in front of the dumpster.

Gracie had spent most of the previous fall in her stairwell home and it had served her quite well. The dumpster and her corrugated box shielded her from the wind and on nights when it did get into the 30s or 40s, Gracie wrapped herself in large plastic bags that she'd taken from trash receptacles before pedestrians had a chance to fill them up.

But, as the rains came, the box inevitably weakened, and Gracie was forced to move. She'd had her eye on 909 Collins for some time but had to wait until the prior tenants—three gentlemen that Gracie didn't like—decided to move on. When Gracie saw that they had gone, she dragged her soggy mattress over and set up her new home there.

Gracie didn't like the homeless shelter across the bay in the city. Too many rules. Too many restrictions. Too many men. She preferred the peace and quiet of her own quarters—be it her stairwell den or her new abode at 909 Collins. But she did make the long trek across the

Part Two: Story-Poems

bridge to the shelter every so often to take a bath, wash her hair and get a hot meal. She'd also look at the dresses they might have in the giveaway, salvage shop.

Today Gracie was wearing her best and only dress—a cotton polyester, black, with a floral pattern. Its camellias, once white, had yellowed with age and infrequent washing. Her sneakers were mismatched. The right, a man's size seven, was red with dirty yellow laces. The left, a woman's size nine, was white and had a hole in its toe. Its sole was detached at the end and would flop if Gracie didn't walk right if she lifted her left foot too high.

In her bag, she carried her other possessions. An extra pair of socks. Men's, discarded at a construction site. A tattered Bible, a notepad, and a ball point pen. A pull-on sweater that she'd found. A chipped, blue ceramic coffee mug. And, most valuable of all, a metal spoon she'd stolen from a lunch counter.

She always carried her possessions with her. They were too valuable to leave unattended.

After carefully scanning each page of the paper, Gracie recrossed the street and started up Ocean Drive. Clusters of people had already formed. The usual parade on Ocean that morning. Quite a few had settled in at cafés to people-watch, the favorite pastime on South Beach. There were roving bands of Latin boys, the usual clutch of tourists, couples holding hands, people together in groups—rarely anyone alone. Except for Gracie. Gracie and a runner, clad only in his underwear, preening his physique. He was blonde, muscular, tight, and clean shaven. "Little does he know," Gracie muttered to herself.

Gracie walked alone. There was a wide space between her and the groups ahead and those behind. For those walking south—walking toward her—they parted or stepped aside, giving her wide berth. Rude youngsters, many on skateboards zipped on past. Some shouted insults as they passed. Often in Spanish. While Gracie was by no means fluent in Spanish, she'd picked up enough to understand the import of what they said. She needed no translation.

"Fuera del camino pedazo de mierda!" ("Out of the way, you old piece of shit!")

"No hay basuraen la acera! " ("No garbage on the sidewalk!")

Gracie ignored their insults. She was heading north toward the Café Cardozo at the corner of Ocean and 13th. Specifically, the last table on the 13th Street side around the corner from Ocean.

If no one was seated there, she'd usually find some money. And always the same amount: $1.37. Five quarters, a dime and two pennies. The exact amount required for a burger and a senior coffee at Burger King on Collins just a few short blocks away. Gracie hoped the table would be empty today. Her stomach was and she only had one quarter to her name.

As luck would have it, a couple had just left the table and a waitress was clearing off the plates, cups, napkins, and plastic utensils. She saw Gracie approaching. The waitress scurried into the kitchen and quickly reappeared to finish up her cleaning. Then she disappeared again.

Sure enough, $1.37 remained on the table when Gracie got there. Five quarters, a dime, and two pennies. All neatly stacked. A little pillar of relief. Gracie scooped it up while walking by.

She never saw the waitress—smiling—watching from the kitchen.

Part Two: Story-Poems

III.

Outside
Next to the sidewalk
1200 Ocean
What once was Versace's
There
There by the street
There were the roses.

Firm little buds
Prime little buds
Tightly bound
Tightly wound
Poised
Proud little fists
Hard little nipples
Unsheathed from their green
Nascent with color
Ready to open
Ready to bloom
Ready to preen.
Others
Open
Already sprung
Already spreading
Spreading their petals

Nubile
Reaching for sun
Slowly
Slowly
Silently spreading
Graceful
Opening more
Unfurling their layers
Spreading their folds
Spreading their petals
Exposing their flesh
Fresh
Moist
Colorful petals
Singing with color
Fecund with color
Promising more
Full
Vibrant
Beaded with dew
Sprinkled with the diamonds
Dew on their petals
Bejeweling their skin
Glistening
Ripe
Kissed by the sun.

Part Two: Story-Poems

IV.

Down
Down on the sidewalk
Fallen
Yesterday's bloom
Yesterday's petals
Elderly sisters
Old
Shriveled
Yesterday's colors
Colors now dull
Brown
Wrinkled
Fallen
Drifting
Discards
Scraps
Scattered

Waste on the sidewalk
Remnants
Cast offs
Pieces of trash
Abandoned
Dried
Crisp

Onionskin thin
Drifting with trash
Scuttling with trash
Debris
Papers
Peels and bottle caps
Scraps of city life
Discards
Detritus of city life
Vagrants
Homeless
Turning
Twisting
Drifting
Scuttling toward the street
Scuttling toward the gutter
Waiting
Waiting
Waiting in the gutter
Waiting for the wind
To gently sweep them off.

BLACK

I.

Matthew Crandall stood in front of the canvas, studying the painting, letting his thoughts meander and flow. His wife, Dorothy, sat a few feet away on one of the benches that museums have for those who'd like to sit for a while. She had walked ahead of Crandall, looked at several paintings that were hanging further on down the wall and now was a bit tired. And bored. She was thumbing through some photos of her grandchildren that she had on her cell phone. *These are the important creations,* she thought. *Those hanging in this museum, those that Matt is so carefully studying . . . they're okay, I guess . . . pleasant diversions if you don't have anything else to do. But the grandchildren . . . now they're the real treasures . . . the real works of art.*

The work that Crandall was intently scrutinizing was simply entitled "BLACK" and indeed, that's what it was. Almost.

It was a large painting eight feet vertically and twelve feet horizontally in a simple frame of gold veneer. And it was black. Solid black. Very black. But with a luster to it, a sheen, so that if you came up to it from the side, it almost appeared to shine. And, if you looked closely, really close, you could see that there were the tiniest dots of color embedded in its black pigment. Tinier than pinpricks. So tiny that

Crandall didn't notice them at first. No one did at first glance. People who came up to the painting dismissed it superficially, thinking it was nothing but black paint applied to a canvas. "This is art?" "I could have painted that." "You mean this guy got a million bucks for that?" Those were some of the typical mutterings of many who observed the painting.

But not Crandall. He marveled at the black, its depth and its distance. Its luster and the tiny, almost invisible little points of color that it held. *A hadal of blackness,* he thought. *Could even Seurat have painted dots that small,* he wondered, *just little needle pricks. Not even as big as that.* And he moved even closer to examine. *Just little atoms of color.*

"Dorothy, come here a minute. Did you see these little pin pricks of color?" he asked his wife. "What technique!"

"Yes, Dear, very nice," she replied without looking up, while continuing to sit on the bench, absorbed by the pictures of her grandchildren.

Crandall stepped back, still staring at the painting, held by the workmanship, the technique. What did it mean? Did it mean anything more than what it was?

II.

Colors
Captives
Seized by black
Captured by darkness
Held by a void
Embedded forever
No longer to shine
Many have drowned
Thousands have drowned
Millions have drowned
Those we can't see
Sunk in this void
Tried to escape
Resisted the pull
But were sucked further down
Pulled further in
A quicksand of black
Smart, tiny sparks
Vivid with color
Their brightness extinguished
Their colors extinct
Their radiance lost
Their preciousness drowned
Consumed by the black
And those that remain

Just Beyond Those Hills

Still on the surface
Still within sight
Last stamens of color
Still clinging to light
Yearning for light
Grasping for holds
Holds that aren't there
Resisting the pull
But drawn further in
Pulled further down
Relentlessly down
Last echoes of color
Drawn deep in the hole
Deep in the black
The fathomless black
Soon to be gone
No longer to shine
Their brightness extinguished
Their colors forgotten
All memory lost...

*

Part Two: Story-Poems

Is this where all worlds go
The fate of all that is
The fate of all that was
All that's yet to be
Where cultures disappear
The Mayans resting place
Phoenicia's final port
Is this where Mozart plays
The crypt of Michelangelo
Is this where Newton dwells
(The fate that he foresaw)
Is this what waits for us
Is this our destiny
Will earth and moon persist
Or will they come to this
Become just tiny dots
A speck of blue
A speck of white
Quick sinking in this black?

And where are all the stars
What happened to their light
Is even starlight doomed?
Does black emit no light
And what about our sun
Will this too be its fate?

And where does all this end
Where does it bottom out
What's on the other side
What planets will emerge
What stars and moons and skies
Will ever gain release
What will this hold set free
What's to come of this
What worlds will it disgorge
What colors will survive
What new life will arise?
Will blackness be the end?
Indeed, what is this black
What is its deep allure
Its onyx heart
Why can't these colors flee
Burst out
Break free
Make clean escape
Are breakouts not allowed
Volcanoes banned?

What is this thing of black
What message have we here
What does this painting say
That all will be consumed

Part Two: Story-Poems

All worlds for certain doomed
That darkness reigns supreme?
Or is this final peace
Eternal blissful sleep
A promised rest
Nirvana yet to come
Elysium
The rapture of oblivion?
Or is it none of this
None of this at all?

*

"Come on now, Matt, let's move along. You've stood there long enough. You're acting rather queer. I'm tired of sitting 'round. Let's get out of here."

BUTTERFLIES

I. The Butterfly
Somewhere
Somewhere from a rainbow sprung
Coming bearing colors
Colors of the rainbow
Birthed from mother rainbow
Pure and delicate
High and fluttering down
Perhaps an apparition
A vision in a dream
Something not quite real
Emerging from the distance
Slowly coming down
Soundlessly descending
Descending without haste
Something from a distance
A distance we can't see
But something coming on
Slowly coming on
Surely coming on

Part Two: Story-Poems

Descending to our midst
With doubt and hesitation
Uncertain where to land
Yet another flutter
Another flutter upward
Cautious
Hesitant
Descending now again
Soundlessly descending
Entering our presence
A gift from far-off rainbow
A gift of lustrous colors
Radiant and pure
Innocent and fragile
Beauty now descending
Gently coming earthward
Earthward where we are
A thing we yearn to touch
To touch but not to grasp
To touch and gently hold
A flight we yearn to capture
To capture and to keep
Cousin of a flower
Twin petals floating down
Adrift and floating down
Twin petals floating down

Then rising up once more
Lifting on a breeze
Wafting on a breeze
Gliding
Swooping
Long and languid swoops
Seductive swoops
Alluring swoops
Enticing us to stare
Enticing us to pause
Searching for a flower
Hovering over flowers
A bank of cousin flowers
Deciding which to pick
Uncertain which to choose
Fluttering its wings
Rising up once more
Then gliding gracefully down
Gracefully down once more
Hovering again
Fluttering its wings
Uncertain which to choose
Which petal to select
Searching for the one
The one to mate and match
Then finally choosing one

Part Two: Story-Poems

It soundlessly alights
Alights upon a petal
A cousin-colored petal
Spreading wide its wings
Luxuriant open wings
Then folding them again
Wings now pressed together
Upright on the flower
Wide spreading them again
Blanket on flower
Gently on the flower
Silk upon the flower
Wings spread upon the flower
Tapestries of color
Luxuriant in the sun
Receiving warmth of sun
Absorbing warmth of sun
Basking in the sun.

II. The Student

She opens up her curtains
Sees the bright blue sky
The azure deep blue sky
Sees the pines are swaying
The tops of pines soft swaying
Gently how they sway
Slowly back and forth
Responding to the breeze
The morning's soft warm breeze
Opens up her door
Steps out onto her porch
Confirms the temperature
Confirms it's eighty-six
Soothing, bright and warm
Soothing summer warm
Turns and goes back in
Reentering her home
Saying to herself
It's much too nice a day
Too good a day to pass
Biology can wait
Brings out a fresh clean blanket
A blanket and a pillow
Paperback and pillow
Unfurls the fresh clean blanket

Part Two: Story-Poems

Printed flowers on the blanket
A blanket bed of flowers
Spreads out her flowered blanket
Smooths her flowered blanket
Smooths her bed of flowers
Her blanket bed of flowers
Sets her pillow down
Glides herself on down
A graceful flowing down
A gentle curving down
A slow glissade on down
Demurely to her blanket
Face down upon her pillow
Back exposed to sun
Back absorbing sun
Tattoo upon her back
A butterfly tattoo
Tattoo of outspread wings
Radiant colored wings
Luxuriant outspread wings
Resting on a flower
Receiving warmth of sun
Absorbing warmth of sun
Basking in the sun
She, like butterfly.

Made in the USA
Columbia, SC
01 July 2025